The Navigator's Touch

"In this haunting novel set in a world inspired by Norse mythology, Ember (*The Seafarer's Kiss*, 2017, etc.) refreshingly places a number of queer and gender nonbinary characters at the forefront, all rendered with nuanced care."

—*Kirkus Reviews*

"The final book in a duology, Julia Ember makes good on the promises she made in *The Seafarer's Kiss* with a compelling fantasy novel about a queer shieldmaiden and her mermaid companion. Fantasy rooted in Norse mythology is starting to feel cliched at this point, but Ember breathes new life into the genre with a pleasingly diverse rollicking tale that gives a nod to J.M. Barrie and sits comfortably alongside fellow queer SFF authors Seanan Mcguire and Catherynne M. Valente. A strong second novel that leaves the reader eager for whatever Ember has in store for us next."

—Kaite Welsh, author of *Wages of Sin*

RAVES FOR

The Seafarer's Kiss

"A romantic, atmospheric and richly detailed take on *The Little Mermaid*. I loved it."

—Samantha Shannon, bestselling author of *The Bone Season*

"A beautiful Norse retelling of *The Little Mermaid*, featuring a young mermaid desperate to break free and a shieldmaiden bent on revenge—dark and romantic, and definitely recommended."

—Laura Lam, author of *Pantomime and False Hearts*

"Dive deep into the dark and brutal waters of the northern sea in this lush, original retelling of *The Little Mermaid*. *The Seafarer's Kiss* took my breath away."

—Heidi Heilig, author of *The Girl from Everywhere*

"[There] is plenty of action (spiced up with romance) to keep pages turning."

—*Kirkus Reviews*

"Original fairytales were dark, and this book is no exception. There's no singing crab to lighten the mood. I am 100% down for that, though. I was more than willing to spend a lot of time underwater in Ersel's world because it was so fascinating. There's a lot of amazing world-building in this book."

—SB-TB.com

The Navigator's Touch

Julia Ember

interlude ✦ press • new york

For Darth Lovely – A book isn't quite as good as a penguin's rock from Antarctica, but it's close.

This book contains some graphic violence and scenes that may be upsetting for some readers. A full list of content warnings and potential triggers, with corresponding chapters, can be found at the back of this book.

(www.interludepress.com/content-warnings)

In the time of legends

THE MAIDEN'S SONG DREW THE god's attention as he galloped over the Northern Sea. The song had a loneliness that called to Heimdallr; each note was hesitant and sweet, whispered to the air. The god peeled back his sleeve and the cobalt tattoos on his arm arranged themselves into a map, charting a course to the sound. Compelled as if enchanted, Heimdallr nudged Gulltoppr with his heels. The water horse tossed his golden mane and surged over the ocean's tumult, toward the source of the god's desire.

Heimdallr imagined a slight girl: alone and afraid after her kinsmen had died in battle or succumbed to the ocean. Maybe she had been captured from a distant land and become a spoil of war, abandoned when her kidnappers perished at sea. Or maybe she was a healer, brought into battle to tend the sick and repair the sails, alone untouched by a plague that ravished her ship. If he chose, Heimdallr could see her safely to shore and leave her with no memory of him or the great water stallion.

She might perform a poem and worship him with her beautiful voice. Or she might be enraptured by his appearance, as so many humans were, and worship him in more carnal ways. Heimdallr smirked. The god had taken human lovers of many genders before, all of them for fleeting affairs, though he never forced anyone. But stealing a god's heart was not a task for mortals. The Norns guarded Heimdallr's hjarta and would not let it fall into unworthy human hands.

But as he drew close to the source of the song, Heimdallr discovered that the woman was a warrior. She sang to herself as she tightened the starboard shroud of her vast drekkar. He halted alongside the ship's deck, concealing himself and Gulltoppr behind a veil of sea mist and illusion. The warrior carried a sword covered in crusted brown blood strapped to her back. Jagged, red cuts and faded, white scars worn as proudly as gold decorated her forearms. She had wild eyes the color of a storm sky and sweat-streaked auburn hair. Her fingers were chapped by cold and salt, but they worked nimbly. The warrior tied a series of knots so fast even the god's eyes had trouble following. With a groan, she pushed herself to her feet and, hands braced on wide, strong hips, surveyed her work.

Her ship was fractured and storm-beaten; its mast was cracked, and its burgundy sail was in tatters. Three large bodies were piled together under a sodden bear pelt. Their congealing blood had seeped from under the fur and stained the deck. Heimdallr smelled the men's rotting flesh on the wind. They must have been the woman's brothers in battle, since she took such care in returning their bodies home. She was putting herself at great risk. Unburned bodies lured water spirits and sharks; they polluted the air with disease and deadly fumes. Her chances of survival were better alone.

Gulltoppr stamped his hoof on the crest of a wave. Sighing, the god stroked the water horse's neck. The stallion would not stand and draw on his magic forever, not with fresh human blood within reach of his sharp teeth, not at sea, when Gulltoppr need only snatch the warrior by the arm and drag his helpless meal into the depths.

The shieldmaiden stared ahead into the space where he waited, invisible, then glanced toward her unmoving sail. She licked one of her fingers and held it to the air, feeling for the breeze. She cocked her head, studied the rise and fall of the waves, and said flatly, "You're blocking my wind."

In surprise, Heimdallr dropped his magic shield. The mist around him dissipated. Gulltoppr tensed beneath him, ready to strike. The warrior's eyes widened at his appearance and she drew the sword from her back. How had she known he was watching? And why did she not kneel? What mortal would not quail at the sight of him? He had heard the desperation of her song. She knew that death followed her ship. And he was Heimdallr, guardian of the gods, a head taller than any mortal man. He swung his leg over Gulltoppr's broad back and stepped onto the deck of the ship. The horse gave a frustrated whinny, but sank into the dark water to wait.

"Do you know who I am?" Heimdallr asked.

The warrior stepped toward him with her sword still raised. She stood only as high as Heimdallr's waist and yet she glared up at him with such ferocity that it was the god who backed away. "I am Jarl Sigrid and you are a stowaway upon my ship."

Heimdallr swallowed, unsure whether to laugh or protest. In his millennia of scouring the earth and the oceans, he had never encountered a mortal so utterly without fear. Her crew was dead; her ship was all but destroyed. She needed his aid. And yet, her thunderstorm eyes remained locked on his; her blade held position at his throat. In an instant, he found himself as lost as the imaginary maiden his mind had conjured.

He sank to his knees before Sigrid. She sheathed her blade. His heart pounded in his chest, more alive than it had been in a millennium. Here was a mortal worthy of Asgard's attention. She would be welcomed among the Valkyrie; he was sure of it.

"Come with me," he said, breathless, and extended his hand to her. "I will make you a queen among gods."

Jarl Sigrid glanced at the corpses, and her mouth pressed into a thin line. She had heard stories of the gods' hjortu, chosen by Fate, but kept in Asgard as little more than decorations. She wanted more than purposeless eternity. "I have a duty to my people."

The god bowed his head. Fate had directed his hjarta, and he was as powerless against the Norns as any mortal. "Then my duty will be to you."

Rising, Heimdallr summoned the wind, and they sailed together for the Brytten coast.

In the years that followed, Heimdallr disguised himself as Sigrid's prized thegn. He muted his god-light and shrank his height, appearing to the other thegns as a battle-scarred warrior with weathered white skin and a graying, black beard. He fought at Sigrid's side and only used enough of his magic to tip battles in her favor, never enough power to draw the attention of Asgard. He slept on the floor of her great hall and feasted among the other thegns. His only condition for this loyalty was that his secret be kept, for if Odin's eye fell upon him and recognized Heimdallr, then the god-guardian would be summoned home.

Over time, Sigrid accepted him as a lover. Her children, she reasoned, should be sired by the strongest thegn, and who better to father future rulers than a god? Sigrid thought that she had forged strong armor around her heart. Despite what she saw of the man who worshipped her flesh, she remembered the stories of the gods. She knew it wasn't safe to love a god, even one who had pledged his fealty. She would not become a gilded prize in Valhalla's vast halls.

Their first child was a boy, strong, but without any mark of divine origin. After his birth, Heimdallr, known to the earldom as Finn, stopped sleeping on the longhouse floor and moved permanently into Sigrid's bed and, slowly, into her heart as well.

Two years later, Sigrid gave birth to a girl. At first, the child seemed unremarkable. Astrid came into the world screaming, demanding attention and reverence, a small mirror of her mother. But a few days later, curious markings developed on the baby's pale skin. Lines of latitude stretched across her chest and legs, and, as the days passed, cobalt continents and oceans of cerulean blue appeared.

When the jarl's people saw the child, they recognized Heimdallr for what he was. They prayed to him and offered sacrifices to Asgard for the miracle. And Asgard responded, sending a legion to retrieve the wayward god. Faced with insurmountable numbers, Heimdallr surrendered. Odin gave him a choice: Return as the guardian of gods to Asgard or live and die as a mortal. After his millennia of life, Heimdallr could not imagine the briefness of mortality. He loved Sigrid, but could another thirty years really be enough time to live? He was destined to exist until the end of time, to fight at Ragnorak. Shedding his human appearance, Heimdallr returned with Odin.

Heartbroken and humiliated by Heimdallr's abandonment, Sigrid prayed to Loki for assistance. She wanted to vanish with her people. She never wanted to see the god-guardian again. Loki answered her call and brought with them Odin's ravens, Huginn and Munnin—guardians of Thought and Memory—to take Sigrid's pain away. She would not remember her love of Heimdallr or pine for him. Loki pitied Sigrid. They understood what it was like to be betrayed by a lover. So they used their powers of illusion to hide Sigrid and her people, so well that even Heimdallr, with his navigator's touch, could never find her.

Months passed, then years. The Norns refused to free Heimdallr's hjarta. Once bound, they said, it could not be given to another. Heimdallr came to realize the emptiness of his long, immortal life. Railing against Odin, he fled from the realm of gods in search of his children and his love. But it was as if Sigrid and her entire earldom had never existed. Though he scoured the earth and seas, Heimdallr could never find a trace of the island he had called home or the human woman he'd come to love.

Knowing that such magic could only come from a single source, Heimdallr confronted Loki. But the Trickster would give him no answers. In grief, Heimdallr's spirit soured. He bided his time. He waited through the centuries for a chance to get revenge on Loki, blaming them for taking his love.

War infested the realm of gods, tearing it apart. In the aftermath, for their role in the conflict and in another god's death, Odin bound Loki's voice and closed their mouth with threads of magic. Only an enchanted silver dagger could break the binding. Odin entrusted the dagger to Heimdallr, who was to guard it and keep it from Loki's hands until their crime was forgiven. But even after hundreds of years, Heimdallr's resentment of Loki blazed. The Allfather had not intended the punishment to be permanent, but Heimdallr broke the dagger into pieces and hid them at the far corners of the world. He used a blood spell and bound his immortal life to its strength, so that, however hard Loki might search, they would never find their freedom.

Part 1: The Seafarer

And now, they are unsettled,
these heart-thoughts,
that drive me to seek out
the high waves
and the salt-tossed tumult.
The desire of my wild heart
calls without relenting
to my caged spirit,
urging that I, so far away,
should seek Neverland
on distant shores.

—Adaptation from *The Seafarer*

Gormánuður
The Slaughter Month
October

A SHIVER OF GREAT WHITE sharks trailed our ship as we rowed through the Trap. Their gray fins glimmered like tiny sails in the low Arctic sun—live vessels waiting to deliver us to Valhalla should we deviate from the course and fall victim to the icebergs.

On deck, another, more vicious, sort of shark waited to devour me. I could feel the hungry eyes of my crew on my back as I squinted into the distant horizon. If any of them could have navigated the narrow pass and rough seas on their own, without my magic, I'd have been sacrificed to Aegir weeks ago.

My crew's loyalty was proving a more resilient beast than their former leader. Haakon had died with my dagger embedded in his chest, but under the thick wolf pelts we donned to keep warm, most of the crew still wore the blood-red tunics of his house. The ice shelf that had been my salvation when I had been shipwrecked was far behind us. If I fell into the water here, even the mermaid who clung to the ship's dragonhead bow wouldn't be able to save me.

Our alliance was tenuous, but this tumultuous stretch of ocean—dubbed the Trap by sailors the world over—had claimed thousands. My men wouldn't take the risk of killing me here. As long as we sailed through dangerous waters, their rebellion would remain locked away, expressed only as sullen glances and curt nods.

I lifted my arm and studied my tattoos. Our route through the icebergs etched its way across my skin. The map stretched from my bicep to the raw, scarred skin of my wrist. It stopped abruptly where the silver hook began. The blue ink of the markings shifted in time with the ship's movements. Miniscule runes detailed ancient, underwater cities and forgotten mountains, lost to the advancing sea.

A frothy wave broke over the ship's bow, spraying us with cold water as sharp as needles. I used my remaining hand to shield my face, but Ersel laughed as water splashed her skin. While we humans shivered under our sodden animal pelts, the mermaid relished the blast of the Northern Sea. She dangled over the waves, unperturbed by the sharks circling beneath the hull. Her eight aquamarine tentacles curled around the forward stempost, and her arms splayed as she embraced the ocean's icy kiss. Her cheeks were flushed, and her topaz eyes were bright with delight.

Shaking my head, I braced myself on the mast and turned to face the oarsmen. "Shift windward!" I barked. "There's a berg ahead."

Groaning, the oarsmen strained to turn the vessel into the wind. The mast creaked as the draught caught the sail. Another wave broke over the ship's starboard side. I stifled a yelp as the cold water soaked through my boots. I pulled the fur tighter around my shoulders and covered my lips with my hand, so the crew wouldn't see my smirk. I hadn't seen an iceberg, but I wanted the crew to keep believing that collision could happen at any moment. Making them feel afraid was the only way I could feel at ease.

I sat beside Ersel at the bow. With a whispered spell, her tentacles receded, and she shifted into the form of a true mermaid. Her long lilac and cerulean tail dangled into the sea. She wrapped an arm around the stempost so that she could float alongside the ship. She had three forms, given to her by Loki when she had passed their test. With an incantation spoken to the talisman she wore around her neck, she could change at will: from mermaid to human to kraken. She thought the third form monstrous—an ugly reminder of what she had endured at Loki's hands—but I had witnessed the sheer, crushing power of her tentacles. I thought them incredible.

I leaned down and brushed a kiss across her forehead. Her skin was cold against my lips and smelled of kelp, fish, and fresh sea air. I breathed her in. That scent was woven into the memories of my coastal home. It reminded me of the rocky beach, fishermen mending their nets at the docks, and the feel of the wind in my hair as I galloped my horse along the cliffs. Her eyes scanned my face. Frost clung to her long eyelashes. With a small smile, she reached up and squeezed my knee.

One of the men scoffed behind us. I rolled my eyes. The crew thought affection for the mermaid made me soft, too sentimental to captain a ship. Never mind that they'd seen me steal this ship with their own eyes. They didn't understand the magnitude of what I owed her. Ersel had saved me from a slow death by starvation and exposure when I had been shipwrecked on the ice shelf near her home. When we'd been caught together stealing a kiss, she had sacrificed herself rather than let me die. To reach my home in Brytten, we could have skirted the Trap and avoided the harsh winds, icebergs, and waiting sharks. But I had promised Ersel that I would come back to repay my debt and to save her as she had saved me.

As the crew looked on, I kissed Ersel's lips.

"The texture of the water is changing," Ersel said after we broke apart. She scooped up a palmful of ocean water and let it drip through her fingers. "We'll see land soon."

I glanced down at my arm and willed it to show me a wider view of our course. The pattern of the map immediately began to shift. For the last few days, I'd kept my attention on the drifting icebergs and the narrow path between them, scared that splitting my focus for even a moment could result in disaster for the ship. But the waves were settling, and ahead I only saw blue. We'd cleared the Trap at last. The icebergs were behind us, protruding from the sea like rows of jagged, broken teeth. *Aegir's fangs*, the crew called them. The Trap was the sea god's open maw, waiting to swallow the unworthy. The sea god was not known for mercy.

Ersel shifted into her human form and climbed aboard. Behind us, my boatswain cleared his throat. When we turned to him, Trygve tossed a yellow, homespun tunic at Ersel. He averted his gaze, and, under his thick brown beard, a blush crept up his neck. I rolled my eyes at him. The men were not adjusting to her. They were afraid of her kraken form and embarrassed by her naked, human legs. Ersel, in turn, didn't understand their discomfort. The impulse to be embarrassed by one's natural body was entirely foreign to her. She understood that we humans felt cold and needed clothes to guard against the wind, but as long as she took her mermaid form to charge her scales regularly in the sunlight, she did not feel the cold as acutely as we did. Even though she stood pink and bare in the blistering wind, her body maintained a higher temperature.

Trygve shuffled to me as Ersel tugged the garment over her head. Of all the sailors aboard, he was the only one I trusted. The boatswain had never sailed under Haakon's colors. He was the peasant son of the fishing woman who had taken me in when I turned up on a Norveggr beach in a battered skiff with only the clothes I wore and a graveyard of fish bones at my feet. They had given me a place to sleep and regain my strength. And when I'd returned from Jarl Haakon's hall, drenched in blood and missing a hand, Trygve had tended to my mutilated arm. Now he did his best as a mediator between our crew and me. He was as broad as a white bear, though considerably better tempered. I felt more confident with him standing behind me, even though I was more skilled in a fight.

He jerked his head toward my cradled arm, then peered over my shoulder to see the map. "Well?" he whispered. "We're getting low on fresh water. Soon we will have to cut the rations."

I removed my fur cloak and pushed the sleeve of my tunic all the way up to my shoulder. The tattoos had finished rearranging themselves. Where moments ago there had been sketched only waves and the outlines of bergs, now a continent wrapped around my elbow. A miniature version of the drekkar bobbed on my forearm, its course mapped with a dotted line to the land's uneven coast. My skin prickled as the waves of ink rose and fell, as the tiny ship's sail billowed in a magical gale.

If the wind allied with us, we could reach the southernmost tip of Brytten by nightfall. Once we landed, traveling to my town undetected would be another matter. After they had sacked my home and taken me prisoner, Haakon's soldiers had split into three groups. One ship sailed with me on board, a prisoner, more precious to Jarl Haakon than my weight in diamonds. A second transported loot—livestock, jewels, fine furs—stolen from my people. The third group had remained to watch for others like me: born with the navigator's marks and cursed to be hunted. My cousin was among those still held by Haakon's men.

Even at night, I was sure that the remaining warriors would have sentries posted along the road that led to the sea. We would need to drop anchor far from shore to avoid discovery, even if that left us without a quick means of escape.

I licked my finger and held it to the air. The wind blew strongly from the east, propelling us toward our destination. I could send Trygve or Ersel ashore as a scout. I wanted to keep the rest of the crew in my sight. The promise of future gold only went so far. As much as I wanted to see my home, I couldn't go ashore myself. I'd bought the ship with my own flesh. No one was going to take it from me.

"One of you will need to go as a scout and make a report," I said.

"I'll go," a young voice piped up from the oar benches.

I glanced skyward, then slowly turned around. Steinair sat at rapt attention. The gangly youth waved his hand in the air; his oar rested across his knees. He was the youngest member of the crew and the most obviously desperate for approval, which made me trust him the least.

"I'll go," he repeated. His breath came in short, excited gasps. He looked around at the other oarsmen and offered me a nervous smile. "I'm small and light on my feet. I'll never be detected. Please, styrimaðr, I need to get off this ship."

A gloved hand cuffed Steinair's ear. The boy yelped and cradled his face. Torstein's oar clattered to the ship's deck. He stood and smoothed his gray hair; his permanent scowl was in place. Torstein strode to the bow; his steps were steady despite the ship's bucking. My hand went instinctively to my hip, where my wolf pelt concealed an axe.

Torstein spared me only a sharp glace before he addressed the men. "I will go ashore. I have the most experience and I'm good in a fight. I know how they will organize. I'll deliver the best report. I'll prepare the skiff now."

I ground my teeth. Torstein had once been a mercenary stryimaðr, with his own ship. He had taken contracts from jarls across the continents and fought in more battles than he could remember. He had the scars to prove it. Most of the mercenaries I'd been able to hire in Bjornstad had been young and inexperienced. But Torstein had lost his knarr on the beaches of Denamearc, when a raid had gone badly. Unable to deliver on a contract he owed, he had been forced to sell everything to pay his crew. He didn't believe in me as a captain, but when I'd approached him at the docks, he'd taken one look at the moving tattoos on my arms and known that I could lead him to the gold he needed to rebuild his fortune and his reputation. Naively, I'd imagined that his experience would be useful. Now I saw it for the threat it was. In his mind, I was a living map, an ignorant, untested girl playing at captain, nothing more.

Steinair's shoulders slumped. He nodded his agreement to Torstein, and the rage inside me swelled. Had they orchestrated this? I wouldn't put it past Torstein to demand that Steinair volunteer, just so he could show his dominance over the crew. My crew.

I gripped my sword hilt a little tighter, then stepped around Torstein. "I will decide who goes ashore and when. None of you are leaving this ship until our course is established. Ersel will go. She can slip ashore and report. Then we will not have to worry about hiding a skiff."

Torstein grabbed my arm. In front of the whole crew, he spun me around like an errant child. He brought his face close to mine. His voice was a growl. "You put too much trust in that unnatural creature. It's Loki-touched. You can't trust it. Bad enough you let it on our ship. I am the most experienced on this vessel and I know what orders Haakon will have given those men."

"It's my vessel. You will do well to remember that." His touch felt like a brand. I wrenched my arm away.

Shaking his head, Torstein spat on the deck. "You'll lead us all to ruin."

A few of the crew murmured their agreement. My cheeks burned. Behind me, Ersel sighed.

I pulled my axe free and pointed it at his chest. "I am the captain of this ship and I decide who goes. Speak out of turn again and your bloated corpse is the only thing that will see the shore."

Laughing, Torstein drew a dagger from his belt. He looked around and nodded to the others. He sank into a fighting crouch and beckoned me toward him. "You think that because you killed an old, sick jarl while he was in his cups, that makes you a fighter? Haakon was a warrior during his prime, but he was a decade past it, and you still lost your hand to him. And without it, what's to say you can still fight at all?"

It was mutiny, laid bare at last.

When we'd first set sail, another crewman, Steinair's father, had risen against me and tried to take command of the ship. But Elvyrn had made the fatal mistake of dumping two casks of fresh water and dried meat into the sea before he drew his weapon to attack me. The crew might have wanted to see me dead, but they had no interest in starving to death. What Elvyrn had done was unforgiveable. I hadn't even needed to draw my sword to defend myself. His sea-brothers had tried him and found him guilty. We'd bound his hands and feet thrown him into the sea after Trygve flayed his back open with a whip. But I had known even as I watched Elvyrn squirm and sink that it was only a matter of time before it happened again.

After that first rebellion, I'd spent many nights practicing with my axe in the hold below deck, dueling the sacks of wool that been stashed there by the drekkar's previous captain. My balance had shifted when I lost my hand, and I couldn't fight with two axes the way I used to, though the hook was a weapon in itself.

As Torstein's eyes locked on mine, I prayed that practice would be enough. He was skilled and strong. He'd been fighting battles before I'd been born. If I died here on the deck, would they all join Haakon's men on the shore? If my cousin was still alive, would Torstein become one of her captors?

I caught Ersel's worried expression. In her kraken form, it would have been easy for her to grab Torstein and wring the life from him, as if he were no more than a washing rag. Her tentacles extended more than ten feet when she stretched them. They were made of pure, sinewy muscle. I swallowed, then shook my head at her. The crew would never respect me if I couldn't fight, and, even if I survived today, I'd still be in danger. I needed to prove myself to them now and be done with it.

"Come on, girl," Torstein said with a laugh. "I won't bloody you too much. We'll keep you alive for the map. You can serve our mead."

The men clustered around us, enclosing us in a ring of bodies. I danced sideways as Torstein lunged at me. Despite his experience, I was much faster on my feet. But the crew weren't giving me room to maneuver. My war-axe had a long handle; I risked hitting one of them if I swung too wide. They were forcing us to fight at close distance, which would favor Torstein's weapon and his brute strength. Maybe they had planned it this way all along.

"Move back!" I shouted.

None of the men took even a step, but then, two long, aquamarine tentacles shot forth and swept them aside like toys. Ersel winked at me and drew her tentacles against her body. I grinned as the self-indulgent smirk slipped from Torstein's face. We circled each other. I slashed my axe through open air. Torstein pivoted, and his outstretched dagger grazed my thigh.

The cut was shallow but salty ocean spray made it burn. Snarling, I lunged for Torstein again. He jumped back, but his foot caught on a discarded oar. He stumbled, and I was on him, pressing the sharp edge of the axe to the back of his neck.

"Kneel!" I screamed, my voice hoarse and wild.

It was within my rights as stryimaðr to execute him. Our law dictated that at sea, I had absolute rule over them, though I wasn't exactly sure how that law applied to stolen ships.

As he sank to his knees, I weighed the merits of killing him against the risks of keeping him alive. Unlike Elvyrn, Torstein was popular. Many of the crew looked to him for instruction and approval. As long as he drew breath, he would endanger my position. But would they all consider him a martyr if I killed him? What stories would they tell of him? Would he be remembered as a valiant warrior who had stood up to a tyrant captain and had lost his life fighting after an unnatural creature intervened?

He needed to be humbled. I needed him to beg. The crew had to see weakness in him before I delivered him to the gods. Torstein looked up at me from his knees. His expression was heavy with resignation, but that was not the same as fear. Keeping my axe poised over his neck, I crouched beside him. Brandishing my hook in front of his eyes, I asked, "Do you know how sharks feed?"

Torstein's throat bobbed.

"They come in groups. We call them shivers for the fear they inspire. They tear at their prey one piece at a time. One bite, then another. They taste you. By the end, there's so little left of your body that even the guards at Valhalla couldn't put you together."

Beneath my axe, I felt him tremble. Glee surged through me. As a girl, practicing my fighting stances and thrusts on the beach, I had dreamed of moments like this, when battle would thrum through my veins and my enemies would kneel in surrender.

"If you ever again utter so much as one syllable without my leave, I'll put my hook through your eye socket and dangle you

from the stern. We will let the sharks eat you from the feet up."
I smacked his back with the handle of my axe. "Get up and go
back to your oar."

Face ablaze, Torstein stumbled to his bench. I straightened
and looked at the rest of the crew. They huddled together. None
of them met my gaze now.

"That goes for the rest of you too! If I hear any inklings of
mutiny again, you die. You think I can't replace you?" I pushed
my sleeves back again, letting them look at the maps on my arms.
"Others would feel lucky to have such an opportunity."

The crew shuffled meekly to their benches.

"If you follow me, I can lead you to wealth none of you have
ever imagined. You will be kings in the streets of Norveggr, with
ring-hoards to make Odin himself jealous. If not..." I shrugged,
trying to look nonchalant, though my chest was so tight I could
hardly breathe. "The sharks wait."

When the crew had picked up their oars again, Trygve came
to my side. "Was that necessary?" he whispered. "Threatening
them all with ugly deaths?"

I looked past him to the dark blue sea and the hazy island
that grew on the horizon. Fear and promise, in equal balance,
that was the only way I was going to survive. To lead this crew,
I had to promise them the world and dangle their nightmares
from the tip of my silver hook.

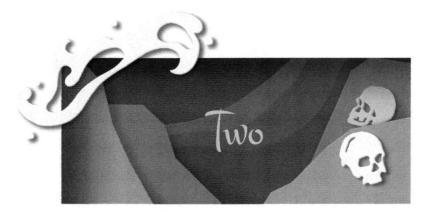

Sólmánuður
The Sun's Month
July

THE DAY BEFORE JARL HAAKON's raiders came, I had visited the beach with my brother, Lief, and our cousin, Yarra. I had wanted to spend the day dueling with Astra under the mountain—and maybe kissing, our limbs entwined, concealed by gorse and shadow—but Mama had needed me to keep the young ones away from the stable. She had planned to give Lief a foal for his name day, and the mare carrying it was due to give birth. Mama hadn't wanted my brother to have any inkling of the colt's arrival until his name day came.

Lief already knew about the foal, but he was staying silent for Mama's sake. He'd seen the new harness in my stepfather's tanning workshop. It was emblazoned with his name in costly green thread and had long, soft suede reins. When I was seven, I would have rushed to tell Mama what I knew, but Lief had a quiet, sensitive wisdom that I'd never possessed. He had wanted Mama to have her surprise.

The foal was meant to grow up with him. Mama had given me a foal when I was six. Fjara had been a dark bay filly, almost black, with a tiny, white snip on her muzzle. I'd spent my childhood brushing her, leading her to pasture, and feeding her scraps of carrot salvaged from our stew. By the time I'd been big enough to reach the stirrup and mount alone, Fjara had been strong enough to carry me. Now she was a warhorse, and her coat had faded to the murky white of a wave's crest.

Mama worried that the new foal was backward. She expected a long labor for the mare. The colt was late, but Innella was a huge mare—her shoulder stood higher than my head—and she was young. Still, Mama didn't want to take any chances. It was the only foal she'd bred that season, and Lief should have had a horse already.

Yarra waded knee-deep into the sea while Lief and I sparred. Lief patiently held up a wooden target for me to strike. My wooden practice sword raised, I stalked toward him. He planted his feet in the sand, braced himself for impact, and fixed his eyes on the ground.

I struck the target in the center. He staggered back a step, then dropped the target, letting it fall into the sand. "You win," he said.

"That's not the point!" I exclaimed. "I'm meant to be practicing. How can I get good enough to travel to Jarl Ivargar's hall if I don't build up my strength?"

Lief shrugged and nudged the target with his bare toe. I rolled my eyes and tossed the practice sword down.

At seven, Lief stood as high as my nose already, but he had no interest in becoming a warrior, despite his promised size. While Fjara and I tore through the hills, looking for caves to explore and abandoned meadows to gallop, Lief preferred to stay near home. He liked to assist my stepfather in his workshop or venture across the courtyard to help our uncle shoe horses. Sometimes I would catch him whittling in his bed, shaping animals and tiny axes long after his candle should have been snuffed out. He liked to say, without jealousy or malice, that I would be a warrior and he would make my armor.

Yarra trotted through the sand toward us. Her beige wool dress was soaked and stained with kelp. She stopped next to Lief and tugged on one of his dark braids. They were only a year apart, but couldn't have been more different. While Lief was tall with deep-brown hair and a dreamer's soft, blue eyes, Yarra looked like a miniature version of me. She had a slight build, all angles, that people who didn't know her called delicate. She wore her white-blonde hair shaved on one side and braided tightly on the other. We had the same warm, brown eyes.

Yarra picked up the practice sword and spun it in her deft, small hands. She pursed her lips and whistled. A few seconds later, a high-pitched whinny answered. His head held high, a golden stallion cantered toward us.

She'd called him Mjolnir, for the thunder god's hammer, and already the horse was living up to his fearsome namesake. He stopped in front of us and pawed the beach before pinning back his ears and squealing at Lief. My brother stumbled back, but Yarra stepped forward and stroked Mjolnir's black muzzle. She had raised him from a colt and now she was the only human who could touch him without fear of his teeth.

"Boost me up," she commanded Lief, who obeyed the little tyrant without delay. She settled onto Mjolnir's back and pointed the practice sword at me. "See if you can hit us," she dared. "That's real practice."

"I'm not going to hit you, Yarra," I began, thinking of what Mama would say if she ran home crying, but then she smacked me across the arm with the wood, hard enough to leave a red, stinging welt. I growled. Mjolnir sprinted away, carrying the sound of Yarra's laughter with him.

I knelt and rummaged through my pack until I found two more wooden staves. Gripping one in each hand, I sank into a fighting crouch. Yarra whirled Mjolnir around. She circled me, and I lunged for her, but the horse pivoted as if born to battle, always keeping Yarra just beyond my reach. My cousin rode as if Mjolnir were an extension of her own body. I never saw her hands or legs move, but the stallion danced for her. It was as if the warhorse and the little girl conspired in a silent language the rest of us weren't invited to understand.

A flutter of jealousy rose in my chest. No matter how I tried, I would never ride like that. If Yarra had wanted to train as a warrior, no jarl would have refused her after they watched her ride.

After ten minutes of sparring, I dropped to the beach in exhaustion; my face was red and sticky. Lief knelt by my side and pressed my waterskin to my lips. I drank greedily, then announced, "She's killed me."

Two black hooves stopped beside me. Yarra dismounted and handed over the practice sword. She smiled widely, revealing a gap where her front teeth were missing. "A worthy battle," she said formally, then tackled Lief into the sand.

When the sun had disappeared, I'd brought Yarra home to my uncle's cottage. Uncle Bjorn had shaken his head at the sand in her hair and Mjolnir's sweat-streaked coat, but I could see the smile twitch behind his pursed lips. "The two of you," he said to me as he smoothed a broad hand over Yarra's head. "Such a pair. Poor Lief."

He gave me a basket of salted herring and a loaf of brown bread. "For your breakfast. Your mother's been in the barn all day."

"I'm sure she'll be grateful for the food," I said.

Bjorn ruffled Lief's hair, then said to me, "I saw you practicing with Astra the other day. If you come by the forge tomorrow afternoon, I'll give you some pointers on your grip."

Lief and I trotted across the courtyard that separated Uncle Bjorn's cottage from our larger house. Inside, the house was already quiet; the candles had been extinguished. Sun-drained, I stumbled to my room and fell into my bed.

It was strange to sleep alone. Until a month ago, I had shared a sleeping space with my sister. But she had accepted a marriage proposal and had moved into her new husband's house down the road. The room was still filled with the echoes of our laughter. I drew the wool blanket up to my chin.

I was sound asleep when a thin scream pierced the night. My first thought was to turn over. Lief often had night terrors, but Mama always went to him. I lay in the dark, staring at the thatched ceiling and waiting for the sound of Mama's footsteps in the hall. When they didn't come, I sighed and grabbed the flickering candle from my bedside table. The air tasted faintly of smoke. Uncle Bjorn must have started early in the forge. My legs shook from sparring in the sand, and I wished that, just once, Lief could comfort himself.

Another scream came, half-muffled, as if Lief held his pillow to his face. He was sometimes embarrassed by being scared, and I felt ashamed for begrudging him. I sped down the hall. Papa often slept through loud noises, but Mama had to be exhausted not to hear Lief's screams. She'd been asleep already when we'd returned from the beach. I'd left Uncle Bjorn's basket of food on the kitchen table, ready for her whenever she awoke.

When I reached Lief's room, firelight flooded in through his open window. I covered my mouth with my sleeve as smoke reached into the room like a clawed hand.

"Lief?" I called, striding across the room and fanning smoke.

My brother was missing. Turning on my heel, I raced for my parents' bedchamber. But a hand reached from the shadows to grab me and cover my mouth. A sword, dripping with blood, pressed against my belly. My candle dropped, extinguished when it hit the ground.

"Roll up her sleeve," a gruff voice barked.

My captor pulled me tighter against his chest and ripped the sleeve of my wool nightdress. His breath smelled of ale and teeth rotting from scurvy. Another sailor, gray-bearded and wearing a blood-red tunic, stepped in front of me. A few months ago, a man wearing the same livery had come to buy a horse from Mama. I recognized it as belonging to Haakon, Jarl of Bjornstad.

The man seized my arm. His eyes traveled the shifting blue navigator's marks on my forearm. A slow, feral grin spread across his face. "Finally. Take her."

"Where is my brother?" I demanded, struggling as the sailor hoisted me over his shoulder. The blood on the sword... I suppressed a cry. They'd come from my parents' chamber. That was why Mama hadn't come. Numbness spread from my stomach up my throat, making it hard to breathe. My parents were gone. They had to be, or my stepfather would be flying at these invaders, his hammer raised. But I hadn't seen any blood in Lief's room. It might not be too late for him. I couldn't leave him behind, alone.

The sailor wiped his sword on his trousers. "Our orders were to take the young ones who showed the marks. Kill the rest."

Lief had been born without the moving, magical tattoos that covered most of my torso and arms. The magic travelled in families, linking back to the god, Heimdallr, or so we were taught. My magic had come from my mother's side, inherited from a distant relative that Mama never wanted to talk about. The outside world was dangerous for the gods-touched, and my grandmother had left the city behind when my Uncle Tor had been born with the marks, hoping to keep her children hidden, safe.

I'd never met Tor. He had been a styrimaðr and had left the village, despite my grandmother's protestations. He had been a great captain—the leader of a hundred men and five ships—until the sea claimed him. Mama never forgot his death, and whenever I talked about leaving the village and joining a jarl's household to fight, it hovered in the space between us.

No one knew why the power showed up in some and lay dormant in others. None of my cousins showed any sign of the navigator's marks either, though Papa often said that Yarra's will was a force all its own.

"It doesn't show up in everyone at first!" I twisted in my captor's hold and tried to scratch his face. "Some people don't show until they're adults!"

It was a lie, small and desperate. The markings showed up in our first weeks of life or not at all. I had been born with small blue storm clouds on my arms; the clouds had birthed continents in the succeeding weeks. Lief was good at hiding. Maybe he had screamed when the men had first come in but run while they attacked our parents. He could be in the stable now. My uncle's cottage was just a stone's throw from the barn. Lief could have reached it. He could have warned them. Uncle Bjorn worked the forge all day. He had muscles like a bear and could wield a war-axe better than any man in the village. He had taught me to fight, against my mother's wishes. They might all be safe.

The warrior's hard eyes took on a thoughtful glow. Jerking his head toward the door, he said to his companion, "Get this one on the ship. Change of plans. I'll get the others to round up the rest of the children."

"My brother?" My stomach lurched.

"Too late for him." The man's hold around my waist tightened. "Don't worry. We made it painless."

I jabbed my thumbs into his eye-sockets. He dropped me with a howl; his hands flew to his face. As blood poured down his cheeks, I ran from my house and into the stable courtyard. I thought of Astra, stirring the dwindling embers of a cookfire in her grandmother's battered cottage by the sea, and of Yarra, sleeping in her bed, unaware of what might be coming. I swallowed hard. It would be too late for Astra. Her cottage was the closest dwelling to the docks. I had to warn Uncle Bjorn. I thought of Yarra meeting the same fate as Lief and grief took away the ache in my legs. I sprinted.

Beyond the wall of our stable courtyard, more men in the same dark red tunics scurried like rats from house to house. They moved silently, never giving the occupants time to wake. They carried war-axes and greatswords, crusted in blood. A few people reached the streets. They tried to shout warnings, but were cut down as they fled their burning houses.

"Uncle Bjorn!" I screamed. Ahead, the cottage was dark, with no light seeping under the door. Scrap metal and stones cut my bare feet; the smoke rising from our neighbors' roofs made me gasp. The horses in the barn squealed and kicked at the boards of their stalls as fire lit the hay around them.

Strong hands seized my arms and hair. I had no weapon, so I bit and clawed. Two warriors dragged me between them, through the streets of my blazing town, to the dark warship that bobbed in our once-quiet harbor.

Three

Sólmánuður
The Sun's Month
July

THEY THREW ME INTO THE ship's belly, an unlit chamber filled
with sacks of dried fish, kegs of fresh water, and piles of bloody
clothes. I screamed curses at them until they slammed the door.
A gangly boy huddled in the corner; his long legs were curled
up to his chest. I recognized him. Vidar was the son of the town
swordsmith and was a few years younger than my seventeen. He
was the only other child in our generation to bear the navigator's
marks, which made him a kinsman of sorts, however distant. He
had his hands pressed over his ears and he rocked back and forth
in time with the ship's sway.

I stumbled to his corner and sank to the floor beside him. I
was still breathing hard. My feet were lacerated, with small stones
sticking to my heels. I wore only a nightdress and a blue pendant
my grandmother had given me, which I never took off.

Vidar glanced at me with swollen eyes. I had known him for
years. He and Lief had been friends, and my mother had taught
him to ride after his father bought a roan gelding with one eye

the color of a sunlit sky. Vidar had never been much of a rider, nor much of a swordsman. If we were going to get out of the ship alive, it was up to me to lead us.

I scanned the ceiling, looking for any weak points or cracks. For any chance of escape, we needed to get off the ship before it sailed too far from the coast. I was a strong swimmer, but no one could survive long in the freezing Arctic waters that separated our island from the continent. The cold water made even the best swimmers disoriented, until they couldn't tell if they swam toward the surface or into the depths.

Vidar wiped his face on his torn sleeve. "They killed everyone. Even my father, who has the marks…"

I nodded and bit my lower lip. It didn't surprise me that the sailors had killed Vidar's father. Unlike his son, Floki was a formidable warrior, as skilled at using a sword as he was at forging them. And he was rumored to have a will as unbreakable as his tempered steel. Mama had always complained about his stubbornness after the town met for council. Jarl Haakon would have struggled to coerce him.

The warrior who had grabbed me had said they were looking for children. They only wanted the weak, those they thought they could compel. I scoffed. I would show them what a mistake they had made. Haakon's fighters had probably imagined that they'd be stealing babies from their mothers' breasts. They'd missed that opportunity by a decade. Only one baby had been born in the past few years showing the navigator's marks, and she had died while still an infant. Vidar and I were the youngest they would find.

I wondered where Yarra was now. There had been no sound from my uncle's cottage. She could be dead, a small corpse lying cold on her bed, fragile in death in a way she had never been in life. The thought made my stomach cramp so hard I nearly vomited. I would have to believe, as much as I could, that she was still alive, that my lie had saved her.

"We have to get out," I said. "As soon as we can. Once the ship rows away, we'll have less of a chance. If we can get off, we can swim to shore and run for the mountains. I know the caves."

"Weren't you listening?" Vidar demanded and sniffled hard. "They're killing everyone. There's no one for us to go back to."

"That's not true."

"Ragna," he whispered, his voice trembling. "It is."

Anger coursed through me, hot as fire. "So they killed everyone you cared about, and you're just going to do what they want?" I stood and paced the hold, kicking clothes and empty sacks aside. "My cousin might still be alive. I have to go back for her."

A pair of sturdy leather boots caught my eye, half-hidden behind a sack of pelts. I grabbed them. They were far too large, made for a man, but I shoved my feet into them anyway. I didn't want to cut my feet when I made my escape.

"We choice do we have?" Vidar wrapped his arms around his chest again. "I don't want to die."

The memories of the warrior's sword, dripping with blood as he emerged from my parents' bedchamber, and my brother's final scream made me shiver. "I don't want to die either." Blinking back tears, I said, with more conviction than I felt, "At least not yet. If I'm dead, I can't make them pay."

*　*　*

WE WERE LEFT ALONE WHILE the ship's crew prepared to sail. Above us, boots drummed on the deck, the shroud creaked, and the ship's stryimaðr barked orders. I found a loose plank and ripped it from the ceiling. The hole wasn't wide enough to crawl through, so I fashioned the board into a weapon. Vidar watched me with wide eyes as I jumped on the plank to break off a shard of wood, then scraped it against a barrel of ale to taper the end into a point. The only way out of the hold was through the door. When they opened it, I would be ready.

"You shouldn't provoke them," Vidar squeaked. While I sharpened my pike, he had made a nest in the corner and used a tattered cloak as a blanket.

"I'm not just going to provoke them. I'm getting out," I snapped.

"Lift the anchor!" A gruff, male voice shouted. "Take your oars."

A heavy metal clang sounded on the deck and the ship lurched forward. I swallowed and sat beside Vidar. I clutched my makeshift pike, but covered it with a pelt, out of view. Anyone who came to check on us would be armed. I couldn't rush at them with a piece of wood when they would have iron axes and hammers. I needed the sailors to come close enough to take them by surprise. I might only get one chance to run.

Lulled by the swaying motion of the ship, Vidar fell asleep. Tears made trails down his soot-stained face. He twitched in a dream. Suddenly, he reminded me too painfully of Lief. I shifted so he could rest his head on my shoulder.

While we waited, my mind churned over the raid. Jarl Haakon's wealth was already legendary. It was said that the jarl had built a burial mound just to fill the hillside with his gold. He had hundreds of warriors at his command and hired mercenaries from all over the continent. A man that rich already, why would he need a navigator? What treasure couldn't he find?

The door flew open. Vidar woke with a whine. I tightened my grip on my pike. A willowy, dark-haired sailor in a blood-splattered tunic pushed his way inside. He tossed a loaf of bread at us. Vidar caught it, but I kept my hands, and my weapon, hidden.

Vidar ripped off a piece of the bread. He popped it into his mouth and chewed greedily. How could he be hungry? After everything we'd just endured? I tried not to resent him for his easy concession. He was still a child, and I shouldn't blame him for trying to survive.

When I made no move to touch the bread, the man narrowed his eyes. "What's wrong, girl? Doesn't measure up to your usual? What your mother made?"

"I don't dine with murderers." I lifted my chin and stared him down.

Vidar made a noise somewhere between a snort and a whimper.

The sailor stepped forward with a snarl. "You'll dine when and where I say. Be a good girl and take a bite. Or I can make this nasty for you. Our jarl won't be pleased if you die on this voyage."

"Fuck your jarl," I said. Vidar tensed.

The sailor stooped and yanked the pelt away. When his gaze fell on my sharpened pike, he staggered back and raised his sword. He had an inexpert grip on the hilt and a farmer's calloused fingers. His eyes were bloodshot; his knees still shook with battle fever. I knew that leaders like Haakon, who sent men on continuous campaigns, required an endless supply of new blood to fill their feasting halls. When they were out of seasoned warriors, they turned to the fields for men. It didn't seem that Haakon spent a lot of time educating his new warriors. This man was new and clumsy.

"Toss that over here," he barked. He jabbed his sword at me, then tried to knock the pike from my grip with his blade.

I shook my head and waited for him to move within an arm's length. I'd never killed a person, but I knew where to strike. Mama had wanted me to stay in the town and breed horses as she did, but that was Yarra's dream and never mine. I'd always planned to make my fortune at sea. With my magic, I could find riches anywhere, if I had the courage to look. Mama hated that. She remembered her lost brother and feared that I might meet the same fate.

Once, Uncle Bjorn had made me a toy drekkar in his forge. When Mama had seen it, she had grabbed the toy and burned it on a pyre, heedless of my cries. After that, I barely spoke to her about my dream. She knew that I practiced and hoped to join a jarl's household and maybe one day captain my own ship, but we didn't speak of it.

"I said give it over. This voyage can be easy for you, or very, very hard," the sailor shouted.

"Why would I want to make anything easy for you?" I spat and lunged for him. My pike nicked his calf, leaving a livid, red scratch.

He thrust his sword into the open air, and I returned his blow, hitting him squarely in the chest with the pike. But it wasn't as sharp as a blade, and I didn't have the strength to drive the blunt wood into his flesh.

The sailor grabbed my hair as I jabbed at his legs again. He fumbled with his sword, then raised it to strike. I braced myself. I'd been raised on stories of Valhalla. If I died bravely, I would wake in the gods' feasting hall and be lulled to a final sleep with mead and song. I'd see Mama, Astra, and Lief again. But if there was a chance Yarra was still alive, I needed to get back to her. I owed my Uncle that, for everything he'd taught me. The sailor swung wide again. I dodged. A smirk tugged at my lips. Then Vidar let out a strangled cry, as the sword slashed across his thigh.

Even though it was not my blood that flowed onto the ship's floor, I screamed. Vidar began to cry as blood spurted from the deep wound. The sailor backed up against the wall, chest heaving, eyes wild.

The hold door burst open. A towering man with piercing blue eyes and a black beard stepped inside. His face was handsome, despite the stern wrinkles around his eyes. He wore golden rings on each of his fingers; a deep black cloak of pressed velvet hung from his shoulders. The sailor lowered his eyes. This had to be the stryimaðr. Looking from his man to Vidar, the captain pulled out his own sword. In a blink, he sliced the sailor's head from his shoulders.

The stryimaðr stepped carefully over the sailor's corpse. Two other men hovered in the doorway behind him, waiting for his command. Their faces were blank and did not betray any surprise that their leader had killed a sea-brother.

"Tie her up on deck," the stryimaðr whispered. "The prisoner will stay within my sight for the voyage."

A thin, pock-faced sailor seized me and wrenched the pike from my grasp. He jerked his head toward Vidar. "What about him?"

The stryimaðr crouched beside Vidar. He stroked the boy's hair, then pressed two fingers to his lips to quiet him. Vidar's face was going pale, and his eyelids drooped. "He'll bleed out before we can help him. Throw him overboard."

Vidar's eyes flew open again. "No!" he whimpered.

"The sharks have to eat too," the stryimaðr said.

"My lord?" one of the sailors asked. "Shouldn't we at least try to stem the bleeding?"

The stryimaðr shook his head. "I don't want to explain to Jarl Haakon how this happened. Do you? Better we tell him that there was only one."

Sólmánuður
The Sun's Month
July

AFTER VIDAR'S DEATH, JARL HAAKON'S men had wrestled me up onto the knarr's deck. They tied me to the mast and left me without water or food. Even though we sailed across the North Sea and the air was frigid, the sun beat down relentlessly and was reflected from drifting icebergs. My hair whipped across my face and stuck to my lips. The sun made me delirious even as I froze. My tongue grew rough from thirst.

When I finally begged for water, one of the sailors brought me a mug of ale. But as I tilted my head to drink, he poured it over me and laughed. "We'll not waste good ale on you after what you cost us," he said. "Jarl Haakon would have paid a good price for that boy."

For the first few days, I tried to follow our course using my navigator's marks. But since the voyage was not of my design, and I didn't desire to go wherever they were taking me, the tattoos refused to shift.

The ocean spread out around the ship, vast, endless, and, for the first time, unknowable to me. I bit a hole in my lip trying to focus on home, and finally the maps changed, only to reveal a bleak picture of my town as it was now. The natural harbor, the forest, and the winding beach all looked the same, but, where my skin would once have borne runemarks detailing the town's precise location and its name amongst the gods, there was nothing, as if it had simply been erased. I stopped trying to use my magic after that.

The winds were strong and they blew us east, aiding the rowers' course. Although no one spoke to me, the crew seemed in good spirits as we sailed toward Haakon's lands. I listened as they gossiped about lovers left behind, their crops, and how Haakon would make them all rich for delivering me to him.

On the morning of the third day, the stryimaðr finally brought me a cup of water. Part of me had wanted to spill it across the deck or throw it in his face in defiance. But I was so thirsty that, when he pushed the cup near my lips, I drank it down greedily. I lowered my eyes and thanked him.

The stryimaðr braced his hands on his hips and laughed. "Feeling better, little one? Maybe you would like to take a walk? Clean up a bit?"

"I want a slab of jerky."

My demand drew another chuckle from him, but he brought me a slab of meat and some small ale to bring back my color. He untied my hands to let me eat and, when I had finished, he allowed me to get up and stretch my legs. As we walked the length of the knarr, the men jeered and tossed crusts of bread and fish bones at me. The stryimaðr raised his eyebrows, but made no move to stop them. Shame heated my face, but I kept walking.

I surveyed the ship: where the crew sat, the little skiff tied beneath the stern, the barrels of fresh water pushed up against the starboard rail. The skiff was the only way I could escape, but untying it before casting off would take too much time. I needed a knife to cut it free.

As we walked past the oar-benches, a man stuck out his foot. I tumbled over, cracking my head against a bench. The man stood and glared down at me. Then he aimed a kick at my stomach. I heaved clear bile onto the deck.

"This is for Bnarin," he hissed softly. "If you hadn't gone after him with that sharpened stick, he wouldn't have been fighting. He wouldn't have touched that boy and he'd still be alive."

He took hold of my hair and dragged me up. He tossed me over the bench, then fumbled with his belt. "I'm going to stripe you bloody with this."

To my surprise, the stryimaðr did nothing. He merely crossed his arms and looked on, smirking. Another sailor sat on the bench beside me and pushed me down. The belt descended, and a searing line of pain formed across my back. I started to struggle harder, but a glint of metal caught my eye. I gritted my teeth against the pain while the sailor beat me, then slipped my hand into his friend's cloak. I carefully drew out his dagger and concealed it up my sleeve.

"I bet you couldn't beat me in a fair fight." I raised my head as much as I could to look at the sailor. I spat on the ship's deck. He let the belt fly once more, and the buckle sliced my cheek.

"Getting your friends to hold me down. Scared of an unarmed girl. Pathetic."

The stryimaðr laid a hand on my assailant's shoulder. I started to rise, but the captain grabbed me by the arm and hauled me to my feet. "If you can't be nice, then you'll have to stay tied."

I struggled and tried to protest but, as we walked toward the mast, I caught the end of another conversation.

"We should look for a whale pod or a white bear before we start back," one of the crew members was saying to a cluster of men, who were all drinking ale from wooden cups. "Fresh meat has been scarce." He grunted and gestured toward me. "And we can't eat her."

"I could find you a white bear," I said.

The stryimaðr's grip on my arm relaxed ever so slightly.

I pushed back the sleeve of my dirty nightdress, then brandished the shifting map toward the crew. "I can find anything. That's why your jarl wanted me, right?"

Shaking his head, the stryimaðr said, "We don't have time. Our orders were to bring back any children who showed the marks as soon as possible."

"A white bear," a younger crewman said dreamily. "I've never seen one, except the pelt the jarl has in his hall."

"It would mean sailing through the Trap," the stryimaðr muttered.

Silence fell on the ship, as the men looked at one another. The Trap was legendary on both sides of the North Sea. It took skill to navigate through the icebergs, but for those who dared, and those who lived, the rewards were bountiful. Arctic foxes and white bears roamed the icy tundra; their white pelts were worth more at market than most warriors earned in a year. Whale pods congregated in sealed pockets of ocean, caged by the encroaching ice. Even a small white whale had enough meat to feed a village for a month.

I turned to the captain. "If you promise that no one else will touch me for the remainder of this voyage, I will get you safely through."

My smile was dazzling as I plotted their deaths. I would see every last one of them sink to the bottom of the sea. If the ship sank, there was only one skiff. Cold, but reassuring, the dagger rested against my skin. I would take the skiff and leave all of them to drown. The sea god was not known to protect raiders, and he favored those who lured blood to his children below the waves. The sharks needed fresh meat; the crabs required new skulls to pick over. If I brought the ship to ruin, surely Aegir would give me his blessing?

The crew members all turned to stare at the stryimaðr. I noticed for the first time how gaunt-cheeked some of them looked. The wealth and prestige that killing an adult male white bear could bring to a warrior was immense. The bears were not easy kills, but their pelts were coveted by kings. Many warriors who sought them out never returned. Unlike the whales, they didn't have predictable migration patterns and they rarely gathered in groups. Their fur blended perfectly with the ice-shelf.

The stryimaðr scratched his beard, then slowly put out his hand to me. "You lead us to a white bear, safely, and no harm will come to you aboard my ship. You have my word."

Glee rose inside me, but I kept my face solemn as I took his hand.

"You will stay by me," he continued. His light gray eyes bored into mine. "And if we capsize as we sail along the shelf, I will drown you with my own hands."

I swallowed hard, then nodded. I would have to pick my moment carefully. Once I led them to the bear, surely they would trust me? A male white bear weighed as much as five men. Our ship was already carrying near its weight limit. The rail was only a few feet above the waves. Weighed down even farther, the knarr would turn only with difficulty, and then, while my captors drank and cheered, I would navigate them to their deaths.

When the stryimaðr turned away, I whispered a prayer to the sea god. I thought of my parents and then of Lief. My brother had possessed a sweet and gentle nature, a quiet voice. If our positions had been reversed, he never would have condemned a ship full of men to a watery death. But because of them, he would never hold a target for me on the beach or talk excitedly about Uncle Bjorn's forge again. He was gone.

I will deliver these men to your children. I prayed to the sea god, *if you help me avenge my dead.*

*   *   *

THE TRAP HAD A DEADLY beauty that took my breath away as we sailed into its heart. I had never seen an iceberg so close. As we ghosted alongside them, I longed to touch their smooth diamond faces. The ocean in the Trap was deceptively calm; the waves merely rippled. The tranquil water gave the illusion of safety. I understood why it had claimed so many.

On the deck, a white bear the size of a horse lay dead. Even in death, it was a beautiful creature, and I felt a pang of guilt for leading the crew to it. Its fur was as fine as powdered snow and looked impossibly soft. Its great black claws were still extended. It was a senseless waste. If my plan succeeded, no one would eat the bear's meat or use its pelt for warmth. The gods did not look favorably on purposeless slaughter. I was glad the bear was not of Aegir's dominion.

Despite their caution and numbers, one of the crew had been wounded in the hunt. He bore the jagged cut on his arm with pride. The captain warned him not speak of the source of his injury. Jarl Haakon needed to believe it had been sustained during the raid on my village.

I had gone below deck while the hunting took place, to prepare as best I could. Immersed in the hunt, no one had minded. The stryimaðr had given me a new set of clothes: a loose-fitting pair of suede trousers, a faded brown tunic, and a cloak made from a gray wolf's hide. I gathered a small flask of water, a bottle of fish grease, a few strips of dried meat, and a long hunting spear. Under the guise of fetching things for the hunters, I discretely stashed my bounty in the skiff to await my escape.

While the men dragged up the anchor, I studied the maps on my arms. Now that I had a plan and a desire, my magic was cooperating again. I shifted so that my back was to the captain. Even now, I had to be careful. We were in an enclosed square of icebergs, with two floating to the south and two others to the east and west of us. The bergs to the south were shallow, small things. The knarr was a solid ship. If we struck them, we might survive. But the berg to the east… it was as big as a mountain.

The men settled onto their rowing benches. The stryimaðr came to stand beside me. "Which way, navigator?" he asked.

His eyes were focused behind me, glued hungrily to the bear's carcass. Did he already have a price in mind for the pelt? He wouldn't bring it to Jarl Haakon. He was probably already planning a new route home, one that would take us past trading ports in other kingdoms and provinces, fresh markets with no connection to his lord.

I squinted at my arm. "To the west," I said and swallowed hard. "If we go east, we'll run into a giant ice mountain."

I braced myself as his gaze shifted. He scrutinized me. I'd never been a good liar, but I was betting he would not believe the truth when he heard it. He'd be expecting a trick now that we had the bear and the rest of the crew were distracted. I could hardly breathe as I waited for his pronouncement.

"We'll go east," he said and turned toward his men. "There're no ports to the west. But I'm guessing you know that."

"If we go east, we'll wreck," I said earnestly. It was the truth, and it was easy to infuse my voice with fear. I was ready to get my revenge, but I wasn't ready to die. My preparations might not be enough. Anything could happen on the open sea. Aegir might decide to condemn me too.

"We're low on water now. We can't make it to the next port west and still get home, not without restocking, and the jarl will know if we bring new barrels aboard. The water is warmer to the east as well."

The ship began to move again, propelled by a crisp wind. She was a fast ship, with a shallow draft for a knarr and a wide sail that harnessed the Arctic wind. Her speed would serve my purpose well. The captain went to stand at the bow, but I hung back. I wanted to be as near to the skiff as possible. We might avoid the ice. The stryimaðr had been at sea for years, and he might have his own accord with Aegir. But my skin showed the full scale of the behemoth that waited beneath the water to the east. I'd spoken true, praying the stryimaðr would not trust me.

I watched my tattoos as we sailed. The miniature knarr bobbed above my wrist, as we drew ever closer to the iceberg. It was marked by a rune, strange for a place that wasn't human-made, but I had seen it a few times with mountains or great lakes. The iceberg could be floating above the remains of an ancient city, still precious to the gods. I gripped the ship's rail. Wind rustled through my hair, oddly warm, like a whisper.

When we struck the edge of the berg, we lurched so hard that even I was thrown back. The tattoos on my arm showed the ship on the perimeter of the ice-mountain, even though the visible part of the berg was some ten meters away. The crew tried to row backward, but they only succeeded in scraping the wooden keel over the sharp ice. A cracking noise filled the air. A geyser shot up from the deck.

The men shouted to one another. Part of me wanted to wait, to watch them in their panic and relish my revenge. But if I was going to escape, I needed to leave before the stryimaðr could make good on his own plan to drown me.

As if sensing my thoughts, the captain strode toward me, sword raised, a scowl on his face.

I ran to the skiff, jumped inside, and severed the ropes with the stolen dagger. The little boat dropped into the ocean with a mighty splash. A board cracked beneath my feet and sea water seeped through the skiff's floor. I covered the small hole with my boot and paddled with my hands, trying to distance myself from the knarr as fast as I could.

My little craft was light enough to float over the waves, well above the iceberg's jagged surface. The captain's face was purple with rage as he stared down at me from the deck above. He disappeared, and a second later a spear whizzed past my ear. I ducked and dipped one leg into the freezing water. I kicked with all my strength.

Behind me, the great ship moaned. The berth began to split from the keel. The white bear rolled off the side of the now-unbalanced vessel, cracking the starboard rail as it fell. Men jumped into the sea and scrambled up the face of the ice mountain. A piece of the iceberg fractured and landed on the deck. The ship's stern plunged under the glassy waves.

From the water, the men shouted and thrashed. I drew my frozen leg back onto my skiff. My calf tingled with cold, but a slow smile spread over my face.

The sailor who had beaten me swam through the water toward my skiff. As he laid a hand on the boat, I plunged the dagger into his flesh. He withdrew his hand with a scream, and I kicked away from him, farther out into the open sea.

When I was twenty meters away, I stopped paddling to watch the chaos I'd created. I knew that I needed to keep going until I reached land, but I allowed myself a just a minute to watch my kidnappers die.

It's not enough, I thought as they kicked through the water, only to be pulled down by a force beneath the waves. My smile slowly vanished. My rush of happiness faded. These men would die, but what of Haakon and all his thegns? These men were just brutes. They hadn't given the order to sack my town. Watching them die didn't bring me the kind of resolution I'd expected. Until Jarl Haakon himself paid for what he had done to my home—to my brother—it was never going to be enough.

*   *   *

THE WAVES HAD CARRIED MY skiff to the ice shelf. My foot had gone numb from hours pressed against the hole in the bottom of the boat. A tingling sensation worked its way up my cramped calf. The Arctic sun beat down relentlessly. I was thirsty, but I forced myself to conserve the little fresh water I'd managed to steal.

When my skiff had bumped against the ice, I'd scrambled out and dragged it onto the ice behind me. If I was going to make it to the continent, I needed to find a way to repair my boat. The shelf was a vast expanse of desolate white. There were no trees for shelter or firewood. Gusts of wind blew cyclones of ice-dust, sharp as broken glass. I pulled my hood over my hair, then tied a rope to the skiff's rowing bench. Wrapping a length of rope around my stomach, I began to trudge inland against the wind.

I walked for hours before I collapsed on the ice. I took out my water flask and allowed myself a few cautious sips. My throat burned, and I wanted to chug all of it, but until I found fresh snow and wood to make a fire, it was all the water I had.

I turned the boat upside down and crawled under it for shelter. As the space began to warm with my breath, I fought the urge to sleep. Those who slept on the ice didn't always wake up. When I'd planned to sink the ship, I hadn't expected the shelf to be so large. I thought I'd find solid land after a few miles. Impossibly heavy, my eyelids tried to drift shut. I pinched myself hard.

Cradling my arm in my lap, I focused on my tattoos. Surely my magic could show me a path. But when the map shifted and my surroundings came into clearer view, I had to bite my fist to stifle a scream. The ice shelf extended for miles in all directions. The map indicated that I should walk back the way I'd come and set sail again. But with the hole in my skiff, I'd never make it to the continent. The land beyond the ice-shelf was tundra; it would be harsh and freezing, but I might be able to use the sparse trees that grew there to repair my boat. I could build a fire and melt snow to refill my water flask. If my supply lasted long enough for me to get there.

The wind on the shelf had grown so strong that a draft blew through the hull of my skiff. I turned the boat over again and was nearly blown down by the strength of the Arctic gale. My lips were cracked and bleeding. I uncorked the bottle of fish grease and, pinching my nose, managed to swallow a few sips.

I trudged on, my whole body aching. The sun slowly dipped behind the horizon and left me in near darkness. Overhead, waves of green and purple light danced across the black sky. When my legs buckled, I flipped the skiff and climbed inside. I slept there until dawn, not sure I'd wake again.

In the morning, I devoured the stripped beef and swallowed a hasty gulp of fish grease. The endless ice stretched on ahead; the horizon was a continuous white cloud. An opening appeared on the ice. I squinted, wondering if I had started to hallucinate. Tiny, rippling waves appeared over the lip of the opening. A spray erupted, and, a moment later, the inquisitive face of a beluga whale popped up. I stumbled toward the hole in the ice. The beluga peered at me over the edge of the ice shelf. Three other whale-faces joined it.

One whale would yield more than enough meat and blubber to see me to land. I didn't relish the idea of eating raw meat, but it could sustain me. I grabbed the hunting spear from the bottom of the skiff and crouched beside the hole in the ice.

The belugas were trapped in a space the size of a small pond. It was the only hole I'd seen in the ice for miles, the only place they would find to breathe until the shelf began to melt. I had never hunted a whale before. On the open ocean, it would have been impossible for me to land a whale alone. But maybe here, I would only have to kill it. The salt in the water might make the carcass float. I could pull it closer and then cut off what I needed.

I waited until a juvenile whale surfaced to breathe. When the dark gray calf drew near, I lunged forward and thrust my spear into the water. The whale ducked beneath the waves, unscathed. Tears stung my eyes. I knew nothing about hunting whales, but something inside me knew that this was my only chance. I was already so thirsty, so hungry. If I couldn't do this, I'd die.

Wrapping my fur around my face to create a mask against the wind, I knelt beside the ice. My fingers curled around the freezing lip of the shelf. The water wouldn't be much warmer than the ice. If I fell in, I wouldn't get warm again.

One of the whales floated just beneath the surface. It watched me warily. I thrust my spear down. Just as the point broke the water, something grabbed it from below and tugged. I lay down on the ice and wrapped both hands around the spear's shaft. But the pull was impossibly strong. One of the belugas must have grasped the tip of the spear in its mouth. I tried to hang on, scrambling to find purchase on the slick ice.

A blue-scaled hand emerged from the ocean. I dropped the shaft and crawled backward. What was that? My breath caught.

A girl pushed herself out of the breathing hole and onto the ice. Her long turquoise hair hung down to her waist. She was naked, but blue scales wound up her voluptuous body. She sat on the edge of the ice and swung a luminous, cerulean tail onto the shelf.

I rubbed my eyes. Mermaids were not real. Everyone knew that. They were fantasies, carved onto the bows of ships by sailors missing home. And yet, she stared at me with such intelligence in her bright, topaz eyes. Delicate freckles covered the bridge of her nose. Her shocked expression mirrored mine: curiosity and fear mingled. She watched me, not moving. I let out a shallow breath, as she slowly lay back on the ice and closed her eyes. I began to scoot across the ice toward my skiff. Without legs, I didn't think she would be able to chase me. I didn't want to be this close.

Her body began to glow. Her scales changed color from deep blue to pale sea-green. Light emanated from them and cloaked her in a halo. She spread her arms. A smile dimpled her cheeks as she bathed in the low, Arctic sun. Around her, the ice started to melt.

I took a sip from my flask and settled down to watch her. The glow in her scales receded. She sat up and stretched. Her eyes locked on mine. Behind her, two white beluga faces popped up from the water. The mermaid bent to stroke them and whisper.

A shiver that had nothing to do with the Arctic wind ran down my spine. Her voice was soft and rolled like waves. She spoke like the ocean and yet, I understood her words.

"You'll be safe," she murmured to the whales. "I stole the harpoon."

I bit my lip. Maybe she had just hastened my death, not caused it. Even if I had been able to kill one of the whales, I'd be stuck on the ice shelf with no way home. The days would grow longer and the beluga pod would break free of their icy prison. But the way she looked at me—curious and a little bit playful—gave me another idea. I needed wood to make a fire and repair my ship. But if I could convince her to help me, I might survive. She could show me how to get to the ocean.

I crawled toward the mermaid. My arms were leaden from days of hauling the skiff across the ice. She could push me into the sea and drown me. What if mermaids ate people? Maybe that was why we all thought they were a myth: Anyone who had seen one had been devoured. But before I could reach her, she dove through the hole in the ice. Her topaz fins waved jubilantly in the air, and she disappeared into the black sea.

Five

Gormánuður
The Slaughter Month
October

AFTER ERSEL WENT ASHORE TO scout, we dropped anchor in a natural cove and waited for her return. So close to the beach, the air lost its bite. A warm breeze rustled the sails and toyed with my hair. The ship hardly swayed on the calm waves. Most of the crew had drifted to sleep beside their benches. They'd huddled together, giving me a wide berth. Trygve and I kept watch.

With her gills, Ersel could stay under the water until she reached the harbor. From there, it would be easy to assess the layout of the town, as the outer walls only extended as far as the shore. She could report on where the sentries were posted and where they kept the remaining children—if there were any left alive. Despite the lie I'd told when the sailors had taken me, I wondered how long Haakon's men would wait to see signs of magic before they started killing. Keeping live prisoners was a risk. Months had passed, and they would be anxious to sail home.

While we waited, I attempted to clean my axe. I used my knee to grip the handle and rubbed a cloth over the edge, keeping my eyes trained on Torstein's slumbering back. He hadn't said anything since our duel, but that didn't mean he wasn't plotting. I was sure my words had made an impression on him and the crew, but I still couldn't decide if sparing his life had been a good decision. He would resent me even more now, and, once his fear had faded, his mind would turn to rebellion. If he hid his thoughts, I might not see mutiny coming until it was too late. My position on the ship would have been safer with his corpse in the sharks' bellies.

I sighed and scrubbed harder at a smear of dried blood. It was too late to change my mind now. The axe slipped from my leg. Cursing under my breath, I picked it up. While I could still fight, some things had gotten much harder since I'd lost my left hand. Sometimes, I struggled to do everyday tasks, like lacing my boots or cutting my own meat. I was learning to do things in a new way, but it was taking time.

Trygve plucked the axe from my knee. "If you need help, all you need to do is ask. It has to be hard, adjusting…"

I glared at him, then seized my axe. "If you want to touch my weapons, *you* need to ask."

He looked down at the deck; a flush stained his cheeks. "I'm just trying to be helpful."

I felt a twinge of remorse. He was always trying to be helpful, but that was the problem. Since the day I'd landed on the beach behind his fishing hut, Trygve had done his utmost to be useful to me. He gave without hesitation and asked for nothing in exchange for his loyalty.

But he never asked me what I wanted him to do. He just started doing whatever he thought was best for me. Before I'd lost my hand, I hadn't minded his impulse, but afterward, his "help" had become more insistent, more constant, more oppressive. Hadn't I just proved myself in fighting Torstein? If one of the men awoke and saw him cleaning my axe because I was unable, I'd lose what little respect I'd gained through the duel. I could command anyone to clean my clothes or a horse's saddle without losing face, but weapons were sacred things. If a warrior bloodied a sword or axe, the warrior cleaned it. It was a belief instilled in every warrior I had known. I would learn to do it myself, but only if I practiced.

"I know." I rested the axe at my feet. "But they can't see you doing that."

Trygve sighed. "I hate that we sail with a crew neither of us can trust. We'd have been better off with just you, me, and the mermaid."

"We can't take the town back without them."

"And after we take it back? What then? You could give the command to Torstein and let them leave. Good riddance."

"I promised them gold. They're not going to forget that."

"They're not going to forget a lot of things." Trygve scooted closer. He pulled a small flask of ale from his cloak and passed it to me. "If you want these men to fight with you, we have to forge a peace."

"We can't," I hissed, then glanced around the deck to make sure none of the crew had woken. "You know what Jarl Haakon and his sailors did to my family—to me. I sail with these men because I need them, but as soon as our bargain is fulfilled, I never want to see any of them again."

"None of these men have been to your home," Trygve said.

"Neither had Haakon. They're still from Bjornstad."

"They're mercenaries." Trygve took a long swig from his flask, then wiped his mouth on his sleeve. "You know yourself, they were leagues away when your town was raided. They fought for Haakon because he paid them. Haakon is dead." He slung his arm around my shoulders. "I thought some of your anger would have died with him."

I lifted my hook so the silver caught the moonlight. "I'm never going to forget."

The drekkar rocked sharply. A few of the crewman sat up and looked around. I scrambled to the bow as Ersel hoisted herself onto the ship. She stayed in the kraken's form; her tentacles splayed across the deck. Muttering, the crew moved toward the stern. None of them would approach Ersel when she was in her monster's form, and I liked it that way. Their fear of her gave us privacy to speak. We could have gone to the hold, but I suspected that they sometimes listened at the door.

I stepped over her tentacles and sat on the rail. Ersel looked at the water and wrung her scaled hands. "We'll never take the town back with a handful of men," she said.

My chest tightened painfully. "What?"

Ersel pushed a lock of her blue hair behind her ear. "Every adult from the town is dead. All of the houses were burned right to the foundations."

I had seen the town on fire on the night the invaders took me. I had suspected that everything would be gone, but still, I wasn't prepared for Ersel's words. How could a whole world and so many lives just be burned away? Everything I'd once cared about had been reduced to ash in the wind. I licked my dry lips and clutched the ship's rail tighter. "And the invaders?"

"They've built a wooden fortress with walls and spikes. I got as close as I could, but there were at least sixty men in the new feasting hall. They know Haakon is dead. They had a flag above the fortress, but it wasn't Haakon's red sigil."

Sixty men? I remembered the day the raiders had come with painful clarity. The ship that had taken me had been an ocean knarr—a study, thirty-oar ship, built to withstand long sea voyages. It had been bigger than the ship I captained now, but still couldn't have carried more than forty men. Only a small group from Haakon's force had remained to watch over the town's children while the rest had returned to Bjornstad. If their numbers had swelled, they had been recruiting and organizing. My hope of an easy battle turned to dust.

The crew was wide awake now. They stared at Ersel and me and strained to watch our lips as the ocean swallowed the sound of our voices. What was I going to tell them? If they heard about the fortress' strength, they might defect. They would know we couldn't win against such numbers. Some of the more experienced ones, like Torstein, might even know some of the men on the beach from other campaigns. They were mercenaries. If there was gold on shore to pay them, then they would fight against me. And even if they didn't fight against me, they could easily dump me in the ocean and sail for home with Torstein as their new captain.

We were so close. Dawn was breaking. I could see the outlines of familiar hills and mountains on the horizon. I knew those mountains as well as my own hand and missed them almost as much. In the valley beyond, a trail of white smoke rose. Vengeance beckoned. Angry, helpless tears formed in my eyes.

"Did you see any of the children?" I demanded. The easy thing would be to set sail, find burial mounds full of gold to satisfy my crew, and then try to make a life for myself somewhere far away. But if there was any hope that Yarra was still alive, I couldn't abandon her. Everything I knew about fighting and sailing, I owed to her father. And the guilt I felt over Lief's death was still fresh and raw, but if I could save one person from my family, some of the pain might start to go away. Yarra and I could start over together.

"No," Ersel said. She sighed, and her brow furrowed. "Not directly. But when I swam under the docks, I heard a couple of the warriors talking about a child who had been sick at night."

I exhaled slowly. My lie had kept them alive. If any of the children could survive, it was Yarra. She was resourceful. She was strong.

Ersel dangled her arm over the side of the boat. Trailing her fingers through the water, she said, "Maybe if we sail back to the North Point, I can get some of the merclan—"

"To do what?" I snapped. "If we were waging a sea battle, they could help us, but these children are inland. What will they do? Swim to the harbor and toss seashells at the enemy?"

It wasn't a fair thing to say, and I knew it. Ersel had come to my aid more times than I deserved, and I'd seen firsthand how vicious the merclans could be.

Her dark blue eyes flashed. "I was just giving ideas. If you don't want my help, I can always go back to the sea."

The threat hovered between us. I shook my head and slid closer to her. I wasn't sure yet what we were to each other, but I wasn't ready to see her go. She and Trygve were the only friends I had, and still I pushed them away. Ersel watched the emotions play on my face, and for a moment, I thought she would dive into the ocean and disappear without a trace.

"I feel helpless," I whispered.

"I know." Her expression softened, and she pinched my cheek with a tentacle. But her eyes were focused behind me, staring out over the ocean. I wondered if she was thinking of her home and all the people she'd left behind to sail with me. I wasn't the only one who knew loss. Sometimes I forgot that. Whatever connection existed between us, Ersel remained because she wanted to see the world, to find adventure beyond the Arctic sea she knew. She had come on this voyage as much to fulfill her own ambition, as to help me.

"Well?" Torstein called from the rear of the ship. "Captain? When do we sail?"

Captain. That was new. I cleared my throat, then shouted, "Ersel and I will get some sleep below deck. We'll set sail again in the morning."

"Very good, styrimaðr," he said and sat down.

Ersel raised her eyebrows and mouthed. "Well done with him."

I hid my grin behind my hand. We would sail when the sun cast shadows on the deck. I had bought myself a few hours to decide where we would go.

*　　*　　*

BELOW DECK, WE FASHIONED A bed out of reindeer pelts and empty grain sacks. *Forseti's Arm* had a deep berth for a drekkar. The hold provided shelter from the wind and gave me somewhere to go when I needed time away from the men.

Ersel's now human legs buckled beneath her and she collapsed onto the furs with a heavy sigh. I closed the hatch door above us, then pushed the ladder against the wall. As far as the men knew, we would sail for my home in a matter of hours. I didn't think they would try to eavesdrop on us now, but it didn't hurt to make spying a little more difficult.

I tossed myself onto the pelts beside Ersel. When she shifted forms, her body changed as well as her legs. As a mermaid, her skin was covered by a mosaic of aqua, lilac, and topaz scales. Now her skin was bare, pale, and subtly pink. The cold made little bumps appear across her arms. A sodden curtain of turquoise hair hung down her back.

She peered over her shoulder at me; a faint glimmer of water was still visible on her coral lips. I longed to touch her, to trace my fingers down the hollow of her back, to kiss along the soft skin of her jaw, but after what she'd said about leaving, I wasn't sure if my touch would be welcome.

She shivered, and I scrambled to wrap a pelt around her shoulders. Ersel stored energy from the sun to keep herself warm. If she was shivering, then it had been too long since she had charged her scales. It was a long swim to shore, through water only a fraction warmer than ice.

"I found these by the docks." She reached into her hair. Ersel often used her curls the way I used a satchel or a belt. She would wind her hair around things, then knot them to her person. She gently teased out a rusted, iron dagger and a small bone figure in the crude shape of a warrior. Depositing her treasures onto the pelt, she grinned at me. "The knife I know. But what is this?"

I picked up the game piece and turned it over in my hand. It was an axeman, used for playing Hnefatafl. The figure's arms were comically large for his body; the piece had probably been carved by a child. "It's for a game," I said.

Her eyes lit up. "Could we play it?"

"We'd need the whole set and the board. This is just one of the players." I pressed the piece against my forehead. "My brother used to carve pieces like this."

Ersel took the figure. She stroked my cheek and collected a stray tear with her knuckle. I leaned forward to meet her kiss. Her touch melted some of the tightness in my chest. Her tongue teased my lips apart. She tasted of the brackish water that pooled in the estuary beside my town and wild heather from the meadows. When she kissed me like that, I could almost forget that we'd snapped at each other. When her giggle tickled my ear, I could almost forget the crew as well. I kissed between her breasts and down her belly. She shuddered as I nibbled the dimples on her thighs.

Sometimes, I worried that I would never be beautiful enough for her. I was skinny, with dull, cornflower hair that was constantly matted from the ocean salt. Whatever magic or trick of nature that kept a mermaid's hair silky did not extend to human sailors. I was sunburned from the sun's glare; my skin was freckled and flaked. She was striking with her voluptuous, full belly and hips, and her soft vermilion lips.

I didn't kid myself. She was no more mine than the ocean. We had a shared understanding of loss and pain, a desire to make our marks on fate. For now, that was enough to bind us.

She circled a finger over the scarred skin of my wrist. "Have you been in pain today?

I shrugged. "A little. Not too bad."

Day to day, the pain in my residual limb fluctuated. Occasionally, stabbing pain would extend all the way to my elbow, and I would have to remove the hook entirely, to take the pressure off my wrist. Other days, like today, it was a dull, pulsing ache that I tried to ignore, but was always there, insistent and exhausting.

I took the figure of the axeman and marched it up the curve of her stomach. Her skin was still damp from the sea and as cold as the ice.

"Your skin is freezing," I said. "When was the last time you basked in the sun?"

When I had first met Ersel, she had told me about the mechanism mermaids used to keep warm. Her scales absorbed the sun's energy and held on to it. Together with the fat in her tail, the energy insulated her against the worst of the cold. Even in her human form, her skin was usually hot to the touch.

Ersel sighed. "When I hang off the stempost, I can absorb some sunlight. But I haven't basked since I left home. I don't dare do it in front of the men." She rolled her eyes. "If my tentacles scare them so much, how would they react if I started glowing?"

"Oh, I don't know." I brushed her hair back behind her shoulders. "They're greedy men. They might think you were a gemstone. Then they'd kill to protect you."

"More likely they'd hack me into pieces and try to sell my remains. Torstein would murder me on the spot if he thought I'd break into diamonds."

"Possible. But he's scared of me now."

Her eyes locked on mine as we laughed together. The intensity of her stare brought a flush to my cheeks. She scooted forward. Then, slowly, she untied my cloak; her fingers whispered to the skin at my throat. She tossed the cloak to the side and slid my tunic over my head. My skin burned when she trailed her lips over my shoulder. I balled one of the reindeer pelts into a makeshift pillow and leaned back on it. The fur was coarse, and the sharp hairs pricked my skin. But when Ersel bent her head and kissed the underside of my breast, and the pelt might have been taken from the softest mink. I let out a whimper.

Ersel drew back; her head cocked to the side. She stared at my chest.

"What?" I asked, suddenly self-conscious. I drew one of the pelts up to cover my breasts.

"The compass," she breathed. "It was spinning."

I dropped the pelt and stared down at myself. Etched over my heart was a blue compass. Runes in a forgotten language decorated its face in place of directions. Unlike the rest of my navigator's marks, the compass usually remained motionless. But now the long arrow spun around, and the runes danced.

Though the needle sometimes quivered, the compass had only spun a handful of times in my life. Once, when I had ridden Fjara into the hills that surrounded my town and a storm struck, felling trees across my usual path. I had been confused and scared, unsure whether to gallop for home or try to seek shelter in the mountains. I'd felt the compass spin, and my tattoos had rearranged themselves of their own volition. The decision was made for me. I'd followed my markings to a cave where I'd spent the night.

It had moved again when I was trapped on the ice shelf, after Jarl Haakon's ship had sunk. My tattoos had mapped a way home, in accordance with my desires, but I'd had no boat to make the journey or provisions to survive it. After finding Ersel at the beluga's surfacing hole, I had prayed she would be my salvation. But when she disappeared into the sea again, I had worried all was lost. Then the compass spun again. For the space of a day, my tattoos had disappeared entirely. In panic, I hadn't dared to move and so I had waited with the belugas until the mermaid came back.

None of the other marked people had had a compass as part of their tattoos' design. Mama said Uncle Tor had a sea serpent that wound up his calf and only moved in times of danger. My grandmother had two spindly wings above her shoulder blades that beat before the snow fell, as if the gods wanted her to fly south with the birds. When I'd been born, Uncle Bjorn had said the compass marked my fate. I'd been born to sail, to navigate the world.

I lifted my arm and studied it. Commanded by the compass, a coast that I didn't recognize had appeared on my flesh. The map showed not my island, but a continent with a forest of inky trees extending almost to the shore.

"Where is that? Do you recognize it?" Ersel asked.

I pushed myself up with a groan and walked to the chest on the other side of the hold. I kicked it open. Maps tumbled across the floor. I'd stolen them from one of Haakon's other ships. Ersel unrolled the first map. It was a sketch of Bjornstad, the city at the center of Haakon's earldom. I tossed it across the hold. I never planned to return to Haakon's territory. Many of Haakon's sworn thegns wanted to see me tried and executed. In their minds, what I had done to their jarl was not justice, delivered on behalf of my home, but murder.

Ersel unfolded the next map. I knelt beside her and squinted at it. The map depicted the world as I had learned it, stretching far beyond the island of Brytten to the distant, warm coast of the southern continent and north to the wasteland of Groenland.

I laid my arm beside the map. Ersel glanced at the two images and shrugged. "It's hard to tell," she said. "I believe your markings are an accurate likeness, but Haakon's scribe has not copied this well. The coasts on the map are too smooth. The sea does not carve like this."

The map was well-labelled, with cities and rivers all named in a minuscule, perfect hand. But the coasts were smooth and unrealistic. The scribe must not have been a seafarer, who would have known that the precision of the shore's rendering mattered more than the territories' names. My tattoos showed only runes, the gods' writing, so we couldn't match the scribe's labels.

I traced my finger along the continent across the North Sea from Brytten. The forest was dense in the land where the compass wanted us to travel. I knew enough of the southern lands to know that their trees grew more sparsely, in tight clusters around rare, fresh water. Our destination had to be in the North.

"There," Ersel said and triumphantly tapped the map. "Look at the shape of the cove."

I followed the line of her finger. There was a natural harbor in the rough shape of a half-moon. Ersel pointed to an estuary. Even with the scribe's imprecise illustrations, the basic shape was unmistakable. A small note beside the fjord read "Skjordal."

I exhaled sharply. I'd never visited Skjordal, but I knew that my birth-father's mother had been born there. My father wasn't godsborn. His kin were farmers on the continent. My grandmother had travelled to Brytten in a rickety fishing boat, after a long winter had killed her family's spring crops. Her decision had been to leave or starve. When she'd arrived in our town, she'd set up a business weaving cloth in the Skjordan style. I'd never met any of my father's kin, but if the compass was urging me toward them, I hoped I could find help there.

"You know it?" Ersel asked.

"My grandmother was born there," I said. "But I've never visited. I know nothing of my kin who live there now. For all I know, they could all be dead."

"The compass…" Ersel's fingers travelled to the talisman she wore on a chain around her neck. "Do you trust it? It follows its own will. You don't control it."

"It's protected me so far."

"Doesn't it make you nervous? Not knowing?"

I shrugged. "It's different. It might be a god's power, but I was born with this. The magic is in my blood. It's part of me."

It was easy to think of Ersel's shifting forms as gifts now that she could freely change among them. Her kraken's limbs were powerful and awe-inspiring; the only weapon capable of cowing my rebellious crew into submission. But for over a month, Ersel had been trapped in her kraken form, unable to shift. If not for her quick wit, and her mother's willingness to sacrifice herself, she would still be Loki's thrall.

Ersel smoothed a crease in the map's vellum, then carefully rolled it up. "The crew are not going to like it. We've sailed all this way. They won't want to turn around."

"Then they can swim to shore and take their chances with the sharks," I growled. Whatever Trygve said, I was through harboring would-be mutineers.

"You need a crew. I don't know the first thing about this ship or how to row it," Ersel whispered. "You can't fight all of them."

I couldn't take all of them on in a direct fight. Even if I still had both hands, there were nearly twenty men under my command, and any one of them might deal the killing blow. If I started a fight, they would shred me into ribbons and join Haakon's men ashore. We were out of the Trap, and they no longer needed me to navigate them to safety. But I had other weapons at my disposal, and it was time I used them.

A sly smile spread over my face. I winked at her. "I can if you're willing to help me."

* * *

I paced the length of the ship as the crew knelt before me. On either side of the drekkar's deck, four, long, powerful tentacles held the ship captive. The scene was like something out of a myth; a story Mama might have told me as a little girl to frighten me away from the sea. The warship groaned under the pressure of Ersel's grip, and the men quivered at my feet. Their eyes were bright with more hatred than I'd ever seen in them, but delight bubbled inside me. It wasn't right. I was their leader; the crew's fear should not make me giddy. But my captors were at the bottom of the ocean, their bones being picked by the fish, and I couldn't continue to punish them.

Trygve had taken the skiff. He floated a few meters from the drekkar. If this went badly, I would jump overboard, and we would float to safety aboard the skiff. We were still close enough to shore to make it, if towed by a mermaid. Losing *Forseti's Arm* would be a blow. If I consigned these men to death at sea, I'd be starting over. But if I couldn't guarantee their loyalty, the ship was lost anyway.

"If any of you move before I give you leave, Ersel will crush this ship to pieces." I pointed to the skiff. "You will toss all your weapons there. All swords, axes, daggers, bits of rope, all of it. You'll get them back when we reach the shore."

"Why are you doing this?" Steinair asked. His voice was husky with barely restrained tears. "We've almost landed. We said we would sail with you."

I bit my lip as doubt gnawed at me. Maybe I should have given them the chance to go with me willingly, to prove themselves. Two of the older sailors stood by the rail; their hands were braced on their axes. I shook my head. This was the way it had to be.

"Our plan has changed. We will be sailing for the continent to bring on reinforcements before we storm the town," I said.

Steinair started to protest again, so I held up my hook to silence him. "If this ship goes down, all of you will die."

"Sail back the way we came?" Torstein demanded. He rose from his knees. I drew my axe and angled it at his throat. "We already sailed with you through the Trap and across the sea. If we can't take the town, you owe us an explanation."

"I owe you nothing." One of Ersel's tentacles inched farther onto the deck and the ship moaned. I tapped Torstein's back with the axe's handle. "I gave you an opportunity to sail under my command or disperse and find other jarls to serve. With me, you know what you stand to gain. I did not force you aboard my ship, but now that you sail upon it, you will listen to me."

"We haven't seen any gold yet," Torstein grumbled.

I rolled up my sleeve and brandished my tattoos for him to see. "My magic doesn't come free. You have to earn your right to riches, and that means following me where I ask without questions."

The men exchanged looks. Then, bowing his head, Torstein crawled to the edge of the deck and tossed his sword into the small boat. The others followed his lead. One by one, they deposited their weapons in a pile at Trygve's feet. Ersel's grip on the hull relaxed and her tentacles slipped back into the sea.

Gormánuður
The Slaughter Month
October

THUNDER BOOMED OVERHEAD, AND LIGHTNING struck the water mere meters from the ship's bow. The fragile peace I'd struck with my crew had not extended to the sea. As we turned the ship for the continent, the ocean fought us. Hail crashed onto the deck like stones hurled from the sky. Thick clouds blocked the moon and stars. The waves tossed *Forseti's Arm* up in the air, then threw her down again like a child's toy. Each time we crested one of the titanic swells, I wondered if the water would crash over the deck and break the ship into pieces.

Ersel had once told me how she'd spent her childhood exploring wrecks and gathering human trinkets. I didn't want to imagine my ship at the bottom of the ocean with curious mermaids swimming over our skeletons. But as the water started to pool on the deck, it was hard to think of anything else.

I knelt beside the stempost and held onto it with all my strength. The men clung to their benches and prayed. Ersel sat inside the skiff, which we had dragged onto the deck when the clouds began obscuring the sky. She wrapped four tentacles around the warship's mast to anchor herself, and the other four around the hull of the skiff. Even with the storm threatening to drown us all, someone needed to guard the weapons. I knew too well that desperation made people brave. Unlike the rest of us, Ersel was the picture of calm. Her expression was almost apathetic as she gazed out over the gigantic waves. Drowning wasn't something she had to fear.

Steinair vomited on the deck, and a wave rinsed it toward me. My stomach heaved, but I kept my mouth clamped shut. I couldn't look weak in front of the crew. Not now, when my position was still so precarious. It was a good thing I had forgone the stale bread we'd passed around for breakfast.

Ersel shifted her grip, and a gust blew the skiff out from under her, scattering weapons. I dodged as a dagger flew past my shoulder into the sea. Trygve battled his way across the deck, opened the hatch to the hold and kicked swords, axes, and maces into the belly of the ship. As he slammed the hatch closed, he slipped on the deck and collided with Torstein. Both of them rolled toward the starboard edge and the crashing waves below.

Two men grabbed Torstein's arms. My boatswain tumbled toward the ship's rail. My heart stopped. I lurched to my feet. I was too far away. Would they let him drown? I knew they resented Trygve's position. Without him, my control over the ship would be even more tenuous. But two aquamarine tentacles wrapped around his waist, pulling him to safety. I closed my eyes with relief, even as a new fear assailed me. My two friends and I had to look out for each other. The crew would not save us.

It had been nearly three days since I'd reversed our course. The storm was the latest in a string of disasters that had begun when Smyain discovered that one of our ale-barrels had been polluted with seawater. We were running low on food, and our supply of fresh water was down to the dregs. If even one man died, the crew would blame me. It would be ironic if we survived the infamous Trap only to perish here.

The ocean took on an electric, cyan glow as another bolt of lightning pierced the waves. Ersel glanced at the sky, then crawled toward me. She peered over the ship's rail and pointed down at the water. It was lit as if a thousand jellyfish clustered just beneath the swelling waves. Overhead, the sky had turned yellow.

"We need to row away from here," Ersel hissed, her voice raw with fear. The apathy she'd worn earlier had slipped. Her gaze darted wildly from the waves to me.

I hesitated. I'd never sailed through the eye of a storm before, but the color of the water didn't seem natural to me. And if Ersel, who had lived her whole life at sea, was afraid, then I didn't want to know what might be lurking beneath the waves. Still, if we tried to row, we might snap an oar. Worse, one of the men could be pitched overboard.

"I can't ask them to row in a storm like this." I dug my hook into the ship's rail to anchor myself as a neon wave crashed over the stern. The crew scrambled back, out of reach. The water glowed like green fire on the deck. I imagined it eating through the wood of the bow, burning us all alive. "If we don't hang on, we'll be swept into the sea. The wind could shatter the mast. We have to save the oars."

Ersel gripped my arm. Even under the blue scales that covered most of her fingers, her knuckles were white. "I can breathe under these waves. I have nothing to fear from the ocean, but the color… I have only seen a color like that in the North Sea once, and it was right before I met Loki."

My chest constricted with fear. Could the Trickster influence the water? Ersel had left her home to escape them, but Loki still believed she had passed a kind of test. They had wanted her to serve them. They had promised to come after her. "The Trickster doesn't have dominion over the weather," I scoffed, trying to sound confident.

"Don't under estimate them." Ersel lifted one of her tentacles into the air. The mouths on its slimy underside gaped at me. "I did. Look what it got me. I was almost trapped like this forever. Loki may have followed us from my home."

"Should we pray to them?" I asked hesitantly. "To stop the storm?"

Ersel's eyes flashed with anger. "Pray to them? Don't ever invoke them."

The sail stretched in the wind and then tore. Ersel was right. Out on the high seas, with only some wood and nails separating us from death, was not the place to try my luck with the God of Lies.

Another wave broke over the deck, sweeping Bjarak into the water. By the time Torstein and I scrambled to the rail to look for him, the cyan waves had engulfed him. I imagined drowning beneath the liquid fire: crawling to reach the air, kicking my legs through a thick mucus, as jellyfish closed in around me, poisoned stingers ready. If I died here, what would happen to Yarra?

"Get to your benches!" I screamed over the wind. "Pick up your oars. We have to sail beyond this storm."

The crew stared, faces ashen beneath their sodden wool hoods.

"Look at the color of the water!" I spread my arms wide. The ocean glowed so brightly now that the mast cast a shadow across the deck. "If you want to live, we have to get out of here."

To my surprise, Torstein was the first to his bench. He grabbed the nearest oar and began rowing with all his strength. His jaw was set, but his eyes had a glassy, disbelieving expression. He knew this was no natural storm. "To oars, lads!" he shouted.

I seized another oar and sat beside him. With only one hand, my ability to row was limited, but that didn't seem to matter to the crew. Seeing me take a position, the rest of them scrambled to fill the benches. I braced the oar under my armpit. We began to row in tandem, Torstein's shoulder brushing mine. The water churned like thick butter.

Smyain began to chant in time with the oars, and the rest of the crew joined him in song. I lost myself in the movement and the music, the fear and the pain. The ship slowly crested the cyan waves, propelled toward the glimmer of blue sky ahead.

Ersel crawled past us. She slipped behind the stern and into the sea. I whirled around. The trance of the song was broken. What was she thinking? Didn't she worry that the waves would swallow her? Was she abandoning us? The warship lurched forward. Abandoning my oar, I raced to the stern. Ersel's small hands were braced against the hull and her mermaid's tale kicked us forward.

The men stopped rowing. The ship shuddered, and a wave broke over the bow, bathing the deck in light. *Forseti's Arm* weighed far too much for one mermaid to shift, blessed with gods' strength or not.

"Keep going!" I called over the wind, but none of the men moved. I tried to scramble to my bench, but the wind kept blowing me against the rail.

"Row!" Torstein bellowed.

The men threw all their strength against the oars. A wave taller than a house slammed into the deck. The mast cracked at the base; the weight of the sail dragged it into the sea. The men shouted, and a few of them abandoned their oars to throw themselves to their knees on deck. The ship moaned, and boards sprang loose across the deck.

Torstein's reedy voice began the song again. A chorus of hoarse, frightened whispers answered. Our broken ship struggled on, and ahead blue sky battled the dark clouds. I clenched my fist so tight my nails drew blood. Torstein was saving our lives, and yet a jealous, insidious voice inside me insisted that maybe I should push him into the sea right now. I should finish what I had started. If he was gone, the crew would have no choice but to follow me.

Hugging the starboard rail, I moved toward him. I grabbed the remnant of the tattered sail and used it to pull myself along the deck. But as I reached the benches, a ray of sunlight broke through the black clouds and bathed my face in warmth. I extended my hand and let the sunlight pool in my palm. A cheer broke out: a cheer, I knew, that was not for me.

Seven

Gormánuður
The Slaughter Month
October

WE LANDED IN A FJORD, surrounded by gray mountains and dense, frost-covered pines. The beach was a narrow, rocky strip, but the cliffs broke the ocean waves. The waters of the fjord were as smooth as blue silk. Kingfishers swooped alongside the ship's bow and a pair of fur seals flipped and chattered in our wake. Still, by the time the ship ran aground, my arms were close to giving out. I had taken my place on the rowing bench again, since the storm had wrecked our sail and we'd lost a crewman to the ocean. My lower back ached from the cramped position I'd had to hold to keep the oar tucked under my arm to compensate for my missing hand.

I disembarked first, stumbling from the ship on shaky sea legs. Inhaling the crisp, wintergreen air, I wandered up the beach. I didn't want anyone looking over my shoulder as I studied my marks and planned a new course.

Wherever we had landed, we would have to make do. The ship would not sail again. I had hoped to coast proudly into my kin's harbor—to greet them as a worthy potential ally, not a weak girl leading a crew of resentful, half-starved sailors. *Forseti's Arm* might never have been a large ship, but she had possessed a certain dignity; a stark, practical sort of beauty. She had been mine. Now, with her broken mast and broken slats, she cast a much less imposing shadow.

The maps showed that we had landed just a few miles up the coast from where I had intended. We would have to cross the mountains, and make our way through forest, but Skjordal was not far away. I breathed a sigh of relief. We were ill-provisioned for a long journey. The last of our fresh water had been polluted with sea water during the storm, and the men had salvaged only enough dried meat for half-rations at breakfast.

Ersel trotted over to me, wobbling on the rocks. She no longer staggered when she walked on her human legs, but she was still learning to run. She wore a spare tunic from the hold—a monstrous, yellow-white thing that hung askew on her shoulders. We didn't have any spare trousers to fit her, and her alabaster thighs were bare. Trygve had given her his second pair of boots. The fastenings were undone, and she nearly tripped over the long toes.

"Where are we?" She asked, breathless. After a life lived under the waves with her weight supported by water, she tired easily on land. We would have to move slowly, even if it might mean spending a night in the forest. The men would complain, but her bravery during the storm might have saved us. Risking the unnatural waves, she had jumped over the ship's rail and pushed us forward.

I knelt beside her and pulled off the seaweed that clung to her boots. It was tempting to kiss the faint contour of muscle above her knee, softened by inviting, smooth skin, but with the men watching, I'd never hear the end of it.

"We're close." I rose and pointed to the mountains behind the beach. "A few miles. But the ship is beyond saving. We're going to have to cross those."

She took my arm and studied the course. My breath quickened at her touch and the compass above my heart tingled. When she was in human form, it was sometimes as if my skin had its own mind, and every inch of it became hyper-aware of her proximity. A smile twitched at her lips when she felt me shiver. She traced the lines of the coast and the dotted trail that led inland through the trees.

From the map, it was still impossible to tell if Skjordal was a small town or a great city. My grandmother had never reestablished contact with her family there, and it had been half a century since she had set sail as a girl. The town could be prosperous, with ten dozen well-fed warriors willing to seek their fortunes under the command of a godsmarked styrimaðr. Or it could be a ruin. Either way, without a ship, there was nowhere else I could lead us.

Trygve led the rest of the men toward us. He tossed a threadbare dress to Ersel. She touched the fabric, and her nose wrinkled with distaste, but she donned it over her tunic anyway. It hung all the way to her feet and had a hood to hide her turquoise hair. That was better. For all the sight of her bare legs was appealing, I remembered how my crew had looked at her the first time they had seen her—before they had learned the power of her tentacles and learned to be afraid. Their staring, hungry eyes had roved over her skin. Ersel was not mine, but I didn't like the idea of strange folk staring at her either.

"We'll have to proceed on foot," I said to the men.

A few of them turned to each other and grumbled.

I pointed to the crumbling ship. "If you think you can make that seaworthy, be my guests. I would have thought you'd be glad to be on land for a spell."

The tide was rising in the fjord. Even from the beach, all of us could see the leaks springing from the ship's deck. The men silently shook their heads.

Nodding, I started to march up the beach. We could easily walk the distance to Skjordal, but what would we do when we got there? We had no ship, no horses, no reputations, and no money to pay recruits upfront.

I straightened my shoulders and walked faster. I couldn't afford to show hesitation to the crew. I'd lost our ship. I couldn't give them any more reason to doubt me, not when they so obviously preferred Torstein. They would follow me or stay here on the beach with nothing.

I heard sighs behind me, but they followed. I pressed my lips together to hold back a smile. With the crew in tow, I climbed up the dune that framed the beach. I had lost my fitness at sea, and, by the time we reached the top of the mountain, my face was red and sweat trickled into my eyes. On the other side of the slope clung dense pines. But beyond the tree line, a cluster of houses and grazing fields glowed gold on the horizon. Smoke rose from the chimneys, and, if I squinted, I could make out sheep dotting the pastures. It didn't look like much, but it was inhabited.

I took Ersel's arm as we descended. The ridge was even steeper this side of the beach and covered in loose stones. I was suddenly glad we'd lost the food and water to the storm. I was hungry, but carrying provisions across terrain like this wouldn't have been easy.

The sunlight faded to a dim shimmer as the pine forest grew so dense we could barely pass between the trees. We dodged between low branches and tangled roots. The ground a blanket of pine needles. The air smelled of evergreen and damp earth.

Ersel stopped to touch one of the trees. Her eyes widened in wonder as she ran her fingers over the gnarled bark. It was an ancient foxtail with a trunk the width of three men. Lacey frost clung to its bark and ice made fragile icicles at the end of each needle. Ersel plucked one of the crystals and cupped it in her palm, transfixed as it melted in her hand.

When she noticed me watching her, she shrugged. "Plants in the sea don't grow anything like this. It reminds me how far I am from home."

I plucked one of the crystals and popped it into my mouth. The fresh water soothed my dry tongue. The water was faintly sweet, infused with sap from the pine. Ersel laughed and took another icicle from the tree. She placed it on the edge of her tongue cautiously, then a grin stretched her cheeks.

For a few blissful minutes, I forgot about the men, the ship, and the invasion. We ran around the tree, gathering the sweet crystals and sucking on them until our foreheads ached and our teeth tingled.

Behind us, Smyain cleared his throat. He was a quiet man, who mostly kept to himself and was one of the few who didn't seem to hang on Torstein's every word. Ersel turned to him, and he pressed a frost-covered pinecone into her hand. She turned it over and then held it to her nose. She inhaled deeply, as if committing the crisp scent to memory.

"All of these trees start out like this," Smyain said. He peered down at her shyly. "If you plant this in the ground, in a hundred years you'll have a tree like this one. You should take it with you. You can start a forest anywhere."

Ersel tucked the pinecone into the pocket of her dress. "Thank you," she whispered.

Smyain didn't meet my eye. He blushed and scuffed his foot on the wet ground.

I scowled. We'd been foolish to let our guard down. What had I been thinking? Running about, gathering sweets like a child? I couldn't afford to let any of them see me like that. Taking Ersel by the arm, I steered her straight ahead. I walked quickly to put distance between us and the crew.

She didn't pull her arm away, but I felt her stiffen. The wonder in her expression slipped, replaced by annoyance as she struggled to keep pace.

"I didn't come all this way to be pushed around again," she hissed under her breath. "I can look after myself. You're acting like Havamal."

Shame heated my face, and I dropped her arm. Havamal was a merman from Ersel's glacier home. Growing up, they'd been best friends and had dreamed of running away together. Then, abandoning their dreams, he had joined their king's retinue. He had thought Ersel would outgrow her wanderlust, as he had, and settle down to be his mate.

Then, he'd caught us together. The encounter was forever burned into my memory. After I'd been shipwrecked, Ersel had helped me rebuild the skiff I'd used to escape. I'd rowed out into the open ocean, with her floating beside me, to test the skiff's seaworthiness.

On impulse, I'd asked for a kiss—a magical, transcendent kiss—and when we'd broken apart, still flushed and breathless, Havamal had appeared. He had given Ersel the choice: Come with him and be his mate or watch him drown me. She had gone with him and saved my life. I knew that Havamal had later regretted his actions, but after the day my town had burned, the memory was the worst of my life. I would never see him as a friend.

"I'm sorry," I said earnestly, and glanced over my shoulder to make sure the men were too far away to hear. "You can do what you like. I just don't trust the crew. Whenever they do something nice, I can't help thinking they are lulling us into security. They mean to trap us."

Ersel sighed. She pulled the pinecone from her pocket and held it up to my face. "Luring us into a trap with a tree seed?"

I looked down. No one on this crew had truly been my enemy, but in their faces, in the blood-red tunics some of them still wore, I saw the shadows of my captors. It wasn't fair to any of them, but I didn't know how to change how I felt. Sometimes, the light would catch them at a certain angle, or they would say something in their Bjornstad accents, or shout, or laugh, and I was right back in my home town, watching the flames spread through the streets. I was on the beach with Lief and Yarra, and we were sparring for the last time.

"I'm sorry," I murmured. "I'll stop."

Ersel cupped my cheek with damp fingers. The action was gentle, but her voice was hard as she said, "Yes, you will."

We trudged on through the woods. Ersel held my arm, but we didn't speak. The wind grew colder the farther we walked from the beach. The ground hardened and a light dusting of snow covered the needles. It was still early in the autumn, and I wondered what this place would be like at midwinter. We crossed a stream, and then the unmistakable scent of fresh, buttered fish filled my nose.

"Do you smell that?" Torstein boomed from the rear of our little column.

The crew stopped. They whispered excitedly among themselves and turned in circles, looking for the source of the smell. A sharp pain gnawed at my side, and my stomach rumbled. After weeks of living on salt pork, ale, and dry bread, I was ready for a real meal. I'd lost weight and had already needed to cut an extra hole in my belt. Ersel was the only one who had eaten well at sea, as she could dive beneath the waves to hunt for herself. She had offered us part of her catch, but it was too dangerous to make a fire on the deck, and the rest of us hadn't wanted to eat raw fish. The thought of well-cooked, flaky whitefish, maybe accompanied by a wedge of crumbly goat's cheese, was enough to make saliva drip down my chin.

We couldn't stop. We needed to keep following the map and find my kin. We had no money to pay for food. A few of the men wandered off in the direction of the food. I opened my mouth to shout after them, but my legs moved with their own mind. I jogged after them.

The smell came from a small, thatched cottage, built between two mighty firs. The little house stood alone. It had the look of a building long abandoned, with boarded windows, crumbling daub walls, and dark patches of rot on its thatch, but torchlight flickered under the door. The aroma of food was now so strong that it made my knees weak. I could already taste the fish.

Steinair and Brinholf rushed forward. They thrust their shoulders into the cottage's door to break it down. I watched them as if in a trance. Real food at last! I imagined coarse brown bread, smothered in drippings and winter berries, the way Papa had made it when I was a child. I would sit in the snow and eat until my belly burst.

A throaty scream broke through my stupor. What was I doing? I wasn't a thief. Pulling my axe from my belt, I ran toward my surprised men.

"Get back!" I shouted.

An old woman emerged from the cottage. She was barefoot and wore a torn, dirty wool dress. For the second time that day, my face heated with shame. My men had been about to pillage this woman's home and steal what little she had. She was helpless. Taking things from her would make me no better than Jarl Haakon.

Steinair and Brinholf backed away, hands raised. We all stared at the woman. I wanted to apologize, but didn't know what I could say. Ersel finally broke the standoff. She reached into her hair and tugged out a few of the sea pearls she'd braided into it. Ersel pressed the pearls into the old woman's shaking hand.

I was so used to seeing them that I hardly thought about their value anymore. The pearls came from clams that lived in the deepest part of the ocean. It was rare for the creatures to wash up on shore in North. Most of the pearls I had seen at market came from the East, where they had a method of farming the clams.

Those pearls could buy another ship. The thought came so fast and unbidden that I hated myself. The pearls were not mine to take. They were Ersel's only connection to her home, and she had only given them away to smooth over our transgression. Still, surely the old woman couldn't need more than one.

Biting my lip, I snapped my fingers at my crew and walked into the woods. Today, I'd come too close to acting like the people I despised.

* * *

We walked through the night and arrived at the village as the first rays of morning sun crested the mountains. I instructed the crew to wait behind the tree line while Trygve, Ersel, and I went ahead into the hamlet. Leading a band of armed seaman into a peaceful village seemed a sure way to scare the inhabitants. I didn't want them alerting the local jarl to our presence, and we needed information. If the leaders here were allied with Haakon, then no matter what my magic indicated, we would flee. I kept my sleeves pulled down to cover my tattoos and my hook. Ersel wore her hood over her bright hair. I hoped we would pass for ordinary travellers.

The village of Skjordal was tiny, comprising a central square with cottages and workshops clustered around it. The houses were single -dwellings made of daub and yellow straw. The workshops were squat, with rotting beams. The central square was little more than a ring of mud. Dirty, underfed children played with a bloated sheep bladder in the street. They watched us with wary, hungry eyes as we approached. I tried to swallow my disappointment. We were not going to find warriors here.

I knew that my grandmother had left this place after severe winter storms had driven the ocean too far inland, ruining the soil with salt, but I hadn't been expecting it to still look a harsh winter away from disaster. The last few weeks at sea was the first time I'd gone hungry. My body was still strong and healthy. In this place, poverty was deep and everywhere.

A small girl ran up to us, holding a bouquet of crumpled dandelions in her hand. Her feet were bare; her toes blue in the cold. "You'd like to buy them?" she asked hopefully.

Ersel started to reach into her hood, but I shook my head. We couldn't leave a trail of sea pearls for our enemies to follow.

"We don't have any money," I said.

The girl heaved a mournful sigh and went to sit on a stool outside one of the dwellings. From her face and height, she had to be about Yarra's age. My cousin had never known hunger— at least, not before the raiders came. Who knew what she was experiencing now? I bit my lip, wishing I had saved some of our ship's provisions to share with the town.

Hoofbeats sounded up the road. The children put aside their makeshift ball and gathered in the square. Trygve tugged Ersel and me into the shadow of the nearest cottage. Three warriors on midnight-black horses cantered into the village. Two were lean and muscled, each carrying a bronze shield. The third had a softer, rounder build and wore a thick, black band of fabric as a chestbinding. The horses shone in the sun. Tossing glossy black manes, they snorted and pranced as the children gathered around them. The warriors carried baskets heaped with brown loaves of bread tied behind their saddles.

The thegns all wore identical tunics: pine-forest green with yellow trim and a white stag embroidered at the center. I didn't know that sigil. Their fingers glittered with gold rings, and they wore matching ruby armbands. These were not mercenaries.

I pressed myself tighter against the cottage wall. Had a jarl sent them? Had the warriors somehow received word of our landing already? I glanced toward the woods. We were too far from the trees to run. Maybe leaving the men behind had not been the smart thing after all. The thegns carried polished steel swords. If we had to fight our way back to the forest, I didn't like our odds.

"I thought you were going to fall off in the mud! The way that mare can spin!" The largest thegn chuckled. He leaned over in his saddle and jovially clapped the small warrior on the back.

"They put us all to shame on a horse," his companion called. He held out his hand to the first thegn. "I'll take my silver now. I told you they'd stay on."

"You were betting on me? I am your commander! How dare you?" the smaller thegn demanded. They crossed their arms over their chest, but a wide grin stretched their cheeks. "Well, at least Warik has faith."

Still laughing together, the thegns took no note of us as they dismounted. The children swarmed them, and older people began emerging from the cottages. The commander removed their helm, revealing short blond hair, a crooked nose, and a rounded chin. They unfastened the first basket from their horse, then almost disappeared as the people scrambled to get close.

Where I was from, it was so rare to see a thegn who wasn't male that I couldn't take my eyes off them. Growing up, I'd always known that earning my place in a jarl's hall would be a difficult task. Even if I was the best fighter, most of the jarls and kings on Brytten wouldn't have allowed me to join their ranks. This warrior's presence and obvious wealth made me curious about their leader.

The thegns began passing out the loaves. More aid was clearly needed, but my respect for this local jarl was increasing. Our jarl hadn't cared enough to send soldiers to stop the raiders attacking my village. He never would exact reprisals, and Haakon had known that. If we'd had a jarl who cared for the small villages in his province, everything might have been different.

Trygve shifted beside me and took a step toward the square, but I held up my hand. We were hungry, but our hunger was different than what these people experienced. This food wasn't for us. Besides, I wasn't sure I wanted to draw the thegns' attention. The hamlet was small enough for all the inhabitants to know each other by sight. If these thegns had come before, they might recognize us as outsiders. Until I knew more about the jarl they served and his allegiances, we could not be seen.

The commander looked right over the heads of the crowd. They had storm-gray eyes, which bored into mine. They looked at Trygve and then at Ersel. A single lock of her turquoise hair had escaped her hood. My breath caught as the thegn's eyes widened. They tapped the arm of one of the other warriors and pointed to us. I reached up to tuck the hair behind Ersel's ear, but it was too late. I knew they had seen. Trygve wrapped a protective arm around me.

We were the only ones hanging back, and my caution had made us more visible. I waited for the warriors to approach us, but they just watched from amid the crowd. When they had distributed all the bread, they remounted.

"We should go," Trygve murmured. "They haven't arrested us yet, but they've seen us. If they don't take us now, you can bet they'll be riding straight back to their jarl to make a report."

I nodded but didn't move. The crowd had parted to allow an old man to pass through. He was so ancient that the skin on his face seemed to melt from his bones; it was translucent enough for all his veins to be visible. He walked with a pronounced limp, and his back was stooped. Most of his hair had fallen out, but a ring of pure white surrounded his bald crown. In his arms, he carried a teal-blue and red woven rug. I sucked in a sharp breath and took a step closer to him. It was the same pattern that my grandmother had perfected and used to weave her famous sails.

With a bow of his head, one of the thegns accepted the rug from the old man. "The jarl thanks you for this gift. We will return later this week with more bread and seed for your fields."

The adults in the crowd murmured their thanks and began to disperse. With a final glance toward us, the thegns turned their horses and galloped up the road.

"We should go," Trygve repeated and shook my shoulder. "Ragna, we need to get out of here. Those riders could come back with an army."

"We need an army," I whispered. My attention was now on the old man. He was limping into a house at the edge of the village.

I trotted toward him, leaving Ersel and Trygve behind. When he heard me running up behind him, the old man turned slowly.

Up close, I could see that one of his eyes had succumbed to the same moon-blindness that had affected my grandmother in her last years. My palm was sweating. The shape of his nose was the same as hers. I felt unsure and shy. I had wanted to meet my kin and hoped for their aid, but besides Yarra, this old man might be the only family I had left.

Now that I saw him, I wondered if he would believe me. I didn't look like my grandmother. She and my birth father had shared Lief's dark hair and blue eyes. I couldn't prove my identity. And my grandmother had fled this village half a century ago. Her memory might have vanished with her. If they were related, he might never have met her.

He looked at me warily and, when I stared and said nothing, he cleared his throat. "Yes? Who are you? Did you come from the jarl as well?"

"No," I took a deep, steadying breath. "I come from Brytten."

He cocked his head to the side. "I don't know anyone from over the sea. I'm a simple weaver and village elder. I barely travel even as far as the next village."

"I think you knew my grandmother." My voice emerged as a squeak. I had never felt so stupid and so hopeful at the same.

He squinted at me, and his clear eye roamed my face for any sign of familiarity. I held my breath, praying that he would see something in me, a trace of my grandmother that would make this easier. But he just shrugged.

I tried to bury the disappointment and not let the hurt show on my face. He didn't recognize me. I didn't know him. It was irrational that my stomach clenched, and a sob lodged in my throat. But other than a child, who might be dead, I had no one left. It was foolish to hope that a stranger might replace what I'd lost.

I shook my head and said, "No, how could you remember her? My grandmother was Aela. She left this town many, many years ago, after a crop plague. It was so long ago. At least fifty years."

The old man's jaw slackened. His eyes scanned me with a new urgency. Before I could step back, he reached for me. His hand closed around my wrist, and he drew me in for a closer look. He exhaled. "You don't look at all like how I remember her, but it's been so long. My memory isn't what it was."

"I don't look like her." I pulled my arm back and hugged my chest. His touch brought me closer to tears. The façade of strength I'd maintained for so long felt as fragile as new ice, ready to crack beneath me. "I look like my mother. My father was Aela's son."

He sat on a stool beside the door. His eyes crinkled in a smile. "Aela was my sister. My eldest sister. This town has never been much, but years ago we had a vibrant weaving industry. When the famine came to this country, our parents couldn't afford to feed all five of us, so Aela agreed to go. My other two sisters died that year, and fever took my brother a few years after that. I never heard from Aela. I always thought she'd been lost at sea."

He remembered her. Lightness expanded inside my chest, and I wanted to laugh. "I'm Ragna."

"Halvag. The last weaver left in Skjordal," he said, beaming. Then his expression clouded. "Why are you here? This town is dead. Just a few families are left now, left behind while everyone else has sought their fortune elsewhere."

"My family is dead." I had meant to make my case sound grand, to tell him that I was raising an army. But the bleak truth slipped out before I could stop it. Looking him in the eye, I slowly peeled back my sleeve to reveal the hook and my navigator's marks. The maps showed the village, the edge of the coast, and the path we'd taken through the forest. The miniature ship had vanished.

Halvag traced a wrinkled finger over the waves, then sharply drew his hand back when they started to move. His gaze hovered on the hook. I swallowed and fought the urge to cover it with my sleeve. I had chosen the hook to invoke fear, not pity.

"A glove might have been more elegant," Halvag said. "But that looks practical for a seafarer. Catch any sharks with it?"

The idea of dangling from the bow and fishing for sharks with my arm in the water was so absurd that I laughed. It was the kind of thing my grandmother might have said. His grin blossomed into a wide smile. I knew it mirrored my own.

"I came here to look for help." I gestured to where Trygve and Ersel stood. "My family was killed by raiders. They wanted to take children like me, with the markings. I have a crew waiting for me in the forest. They will come when I signal them."

Halvag pointed to his cottage. "I don't have much, but you are welcome to stay here for a night or two before you continue your journey. I can't feed many men for long, but you are welcome any time. I am an old man and don't get many visitors."

"Who were those warriors who came through here?"

"Jarl Honor's thegns. They come one or twice a week to bring some supplies and food. Sometimes they bring seeds. They're helping us rebuild this place."

"Does the jarl have an alliance with any of the earldoms in Norveggr? With… Haakon?"

"We have no love for the late Haakon here if that's what you mean," Halvag said. "No one in this earldom was sad to learn that he was dead. He has raided coastal towns like this one for years." Halvag spat on the ground. "Jarl Honor is fair and would listen to you. If you want to seek aid in Djalsfor, I will see you on your way in the morning. You can say that you are my kin."

"Thank you," I whispered.

My kin. Ducking my head, I bit the inside of my cheek to hide my smile. I walked toward the tree line to signal the crew.

Gormánuður
The Slaughter Month
October

AT MY BECKONING, TORSTEIN LED the crew forth. Now that Jarl Honor's thegns had fed them, the village children seemed to wake up and take notice of the armed strangers infiltrating their quiet town. The bold ones lined the street, shouting questions and insults, while the shy peered out behind half-closed doors.

My men ignored them until a scrappy, blond boy threw a rock at Steinair. Torstein marched toward the boy, and my heart leapt into my mouth as I imagined him striking the child or drawing a weapon. Instead, he knelt beside the boy and produced a makeshift slingshot from the pouch at his waist. With his hands, the big sailor mimed taking aim and shooting a rock at Steinair's behind. The boy took it and ran to show his sister; his round face was lit with wild joy.

With so few people left and no walls or watch towers, I wondered what the village would have done if we had been invaders. Halvag had already mentioned that Haakon had raided it. When I met with Jarl Honor, I would have to speak to him about the hamlet's protection. My town had once possessed a strong wooden wall, and we'd had many trained fighters. Even that hadn't been enough. I didn't like the idea of Halvag living somewhere so vulnerable.

My kinsman had a small barn behind his cottage. The crew was to share accommodation with a pair of shaggy, dun ponies. Halvag offered me a pallet in the cottage by his smoky fire, but I wanted to keep an eye on the men. I didn't trust them not to steal.

As we bedded down with fresh, sweet-smelling straw, Halvag brought us a kettle of thick porridge. We all tucked in greedily, slopping up the mixture with our hands. It wasn't seasoned or topped with honey, the way Mama would have made it, but the hot gruel stuck to my bones nonetheless. We sat in the soft, warm straw and ate until our stomachs hurt. It was the most comfortable I'd been in weeks.

Ersel did not eat. I scooped porridge into a wooden bowl for her, but she wrinkled her nose and insisted that a mermaid could not eat mush made from land-plants. She would find a stream or a lake as we travelled. There had to be fish somewhere. While we ate, she fussed over the ponies. Whispering softly to them, she stroked their velvet muzzles and braided their ivory and black manes.

When I had finished, I wiped my hand on clean straw and went to her. At sea, it had been easy to forget just how little Ersel knew of our human world, but here, her astonishment was plain in the grin stretching her face. I ran my hand down a pony's flank and lifted his rear hoof.

Ersel crouched and peered at the metal shoe on the pony's foot. She laughed and tapped the metal with her knuckles. "You told me about these!"

When we had tested my skiff after the shipwreck, Ersel had brought a collection of her human treasures to my boat. She'd searched through decaying hulls of old wrecks for years and hoarded the goods she found, never knowing the purpose of most of the items she kept hidden. One of the things had been a rusted horseshoe. I remembered the look of horror on her face when I had explained how they were nailed to the animal's foot. She had envisioned horses as huge, vicious creatures, like white bears, that we humans tortured into subjugation.

I pressed on the frog of the pony's hoof. He turned to eye me curiously, then butted his head against my rear.

"He doesn't seem to be in any pain," Ersel said. "Were these like the horses your mother raised?"

I tried and failed to stifle a giggle. Her cheeks warmed. "My mother bred warhorses." I straightened and gently scratched the pony's withers with the tip of my hook. His lower lip wobbled with pleasure. "These ponies pull carts and ploughs."

"Still," Trygve said. He stood and walked over to us. "It might be better for you to borrow one of them, rather than walk to see the jarl. You don't want to arrive exhausted."

"That would be a disgrace," I began, but Ersel grabbed hold of my arm.

"Boost me up!" she demanded excitedly. "I want to see what it's like to ride one!"

"You're hardly steady on foot," Trgyve protested. "You don't just sit on a horse. You have to keep your balance."

Ersel stuck her tongue out at him. "If I feel I'm about to fall, I can always shift forms and grip with my tentacles. It can't be harder than riding the stemposts."

"I'm sure the pony would love that," I drawled and rolled my eyes. I could imagine the little horse's reaction to Ersel suddenly shapeshifting into a kraken and grabbing at him with her long, aquamarine limbs.

"Lift one of your legs and bend your knee," Trygve said. She did as he instructed, and he boosted her onto the pony's back.

Ersel wrapped a lock of the pony's long mane around her hand. "He's beautiful. I'd love to know what it's like to ride them when they run. I bet the wind is amazing."

"Nothing like it, lass," Torstein piped up. He lay flat in the straw, his eyes half-closed. Most of the crew had finished their porridge and gone straight to sleep. "You should ride tomorrow. The old man won't miss these two for a few days. It's nearly winter. The ground is frozen. No ploughing to be done."

I shot him a glare. Of course, Torstein would love for me to look ridiculous when I met our potential allies.

"Please?" Ersel asked.

I hesitated. We had already lost our ship. Our clothes were dirty and smelled of fish and mildew. Mama would say that riding a cart pony to meet an important contact was a disgrace, but she was gone and my Fjara was a hundred miles across the sea. Other than our magic, we had nothing to offer the jarl.

As a girl, when I'd imagined myself captaining my own crew and sailing across the world, I'd always been well-dressed, respected, important. But many of my men would need new weapons and clothes. Our experience at sea was nothing like what I'd daydreamed for so many years. What was one more embarrassment if it would please the mermaid peering down at me with such beseeching, beautiful eyes?

"Fine!" I said. "But if you get tired on the road, don't blame me."

*   *   *

HALVAG WOKE US AT DAWN. The old man rapped sharply on the barn door and then pushed it open without waiting. He wrung his hands and glanced toward the house while I sat up and rubbed my eyes. Pressed against Ersel's soft body, warm in the dry straw, I'd had my best sleep since I was captured months ago. Waking didn't come easily. I blinked at Halvag in the orange morning light.

"The jarl has sent messengers." His words cut through my grogginess, and I was on my feet in an instant.

"What kind of messengers?" I asked, my body tensing with fear. A young courier was different than a cohort of warriors sent to arrest us. If the jarl had sent an army, we weren't in condition to fight. A glassless window at the rear of the barn led to the forest beyond. If we could make it into the cover of the trees, armed horsemen would have trouble pursuing us at speed. But the forest was across a pasture. If the horsemen saw us flee and gave chase, we would be cut down as we ran.

Had Halvag alerted the jarl we were staying here? The thought made my chest hurt, but maybe everything he'd said yesterday about being my kin had been a ruse. If this Jarl Honor had been allied to Haakon, there might be a price on our heads. I'd been a fool to trust Halvag so easily. Without thinking, I raised my hook like a knife. Halvag took a step back. Behind me, the men clambered to their feet.

"The jarl's húskarl." Halvag raised a placating hand. "They were here yesterday, passing out bread to the children. It will be all right. They are alone."

I lowered my hook. "Sorry. It's been a long journey."

Halvag squeezed my hand. "I've found a part of my family. I'm old and I don't take that for granted. It'll take more than that to scare me off."

"Stay here," I said to my men.

Ersel rose from her straw nest and took my other arm. She didn't bother to cover her hair. The long blue locks gave her away instantly as someone not of our world, but, unlike raised steel, there was nothing overtly threatening about her, for all she was the strongest weapon I had. I'd seen the gleam of the húskarl's polished sword dangling from their belt as they dismounted. One did not rise to be a jarl's second-in-command without cause. There was a chance the warrior could best five of us with a blade, but I doubted they would have trained to face a kraken's powerful limbs.

We followed Halvag through his weaving workshop at the rear of the cottage. The pile of thick, unwashed wool, discarded combs, and the wooden loom leaning against the wall all reminded me of my grandmother. The room smelled faintly of dyes and vinegar. I wanted to run my hands through the wool and sit beside Halvag while he worked. I would comb the wool fibers until they were as soft as kitten's fur, as I had done as a little girl with my grandmother. I averted my eyes to keep the memories at bay and marched into the cottage.

The húskarl sat on Halvag's lone chair, warming their hands on the open fire built in a pit in the middle of the room. Halvag gestured for us to sit on the bed, while he busied himself with a pot suspended over the flames. Today, the warrior appeared in more casual clothing, without the jarl's official tunic and sigil. They wore a simple, brown wool dress without a chest-binding. A thick, black leather belt that bore a set of sharpened daggers encircled their waist.

"I am Aslaug." They smoothed a crease in their dress. They stared openly at Ersel. "Húskarl to Jarl Honor of Dalsfjor. The jarl's scouts reported your ship's landing at the beach. We have kept watch over you and your men since, and the jarl is curious about your purpose here. I have been sent to bring you to the city as our guests."

"Bring us?" I demanded. "Are we under arrest?"

Aslaug pursed their lips. "No, but we would prefer that you come as asked. The jarl will grow suspicious if you refuse our invitation. You have nothing to fear."

Halvag passed each of us a steaming wooden bowl, filled with more of the hot porridge he'd offered us last night. A night of hunger must have changed Ersel's mind about waiting for food, because she accepted the bowl from Halvag, albeit with a discontented sniff.

I brought the bowl to my lips and took a sip. "We're here to seek help. As your scout must have told you, our ship has been wrecked. Halvag is my kinsman. He tells me that your jarl was not a friend of the recently deceased Haakon?"

Aslaug inclined their head formally, but I didn't miss the way their jaw tightened at Haakon's name. Whatever relationship

Haakon had had with their jarl, it had not been warm. "We were not."

"Jarl Haakon sent men to my town. They killed almost everyone." I pushed back my sleeve, allowing Aslaug to see both my hook and my tattoos. They leaned forward and craned to see the markings. The blue-ink trees were blowing nearly sideways, as if bending in a strong winter wind.

"I am alive because Haakon wanted my magic." I let the sleeve fall back into place. I wanted them to focus on what I was saying, not my tattoos or my hook. "Warriors still guard my town. They have taken children as prisoners. Our jarl is weak and wouldn't protect us. He won't attempt to take the town back while fighters remain. I have a small crew—but they are mercenaries. They used to serve Haakon, but defected to me when I offered them gold. We need help. I would prefer to sail alongside allies."

"Jarl Haakon was not a kind man, neither to his enemies or to most that served him. It does not surprise me to learn that his men defected easily. But if you are not yet certain of your own crew, how can we be certain of you?"

My face went red; I was angry and embarrassed at the same time. They were judging me, when I had made the best of an impossible situation. How dare they? Weren't they impressed that I'd managed on my own for weeks, despite the hostility of my men?

"Yes, they were Haakon's men," I spat. "But I persuaded them this far, and they didn't drown me at sea. I can keep them in line. We sailed through the Trap."

Aslaug calmly sipped their porridge, then cradled the warm bowl against their stomach. "You'll have to speak to the jarl and explain. I cannot make any decision. I am here as escort only."

I jerked my head toward Ersel. She was noisily draining her bowl, apparently having discovered a taste for cooked oats. "And I have another sort of weapon."

The húskarl's gray eyes fixed on Ersel. "Show me."

Part of me hated putting her on display, as if she really were a weapon and not a person that I cared about. But I had to keep my goal in mind. If getting to Yarra meant making Ersel play a part, then I would do it. She would understand. We were allies. "Show them."

Ersel's fingers trembled as she reached for the talisman she wore around her neck. Her eyes fixed on the daggers hanging from Aslaug's belt. She whispered the incantation, so softly the words sounded like a hiss. Then her body slowly shifted; her legs split open and her dress ripped. From her waist, eight long tentacles grew like vines, knocking her bowl aside as they spread to fill the room. From her pale white skin, scales erupted, shimmering like glass in the firelight.

"Magnificent." Aslaug cleared their throat. "The jarl will be impressed by her, but one shapeshifter isn't enough to win battles, or you would have taken your home back already. Your own navigation might prove useful as well. Gather your crew. I will escort you to meet Honor."

Nine

Ylir
Odin's Month
November

As an apology to Ersel, I kept my promise to ride the ponies to Djalsfor. Aslaug led the way on their black warhorse, with Trygve sitting behind them on the mare. Ersel and I followed on the shaggy, sure-footed ponies. The men had to walk, and I could hear them grumbling.

My feet felt too close to the ground. The pony couldn't have been taller than thirteen hands, with a belly so round riding him was like trying to ride an ale barrel through an ocean storm. But Ersel was delighted with her mount. She talked to him and stroked his neck and ignored me when I tried to point out new human things on the road.

We took the only road leading from the village. It led us through other towns and hamlets, which became increasingly prosperous as we moved away from the coast. Farther inland, the wind had less bite, and the ground was padded with lush, green grass. Cattle and sheep grazed the fields along the road. As we rode, the cheeks of the onlookers seemed to grow fuller too.

Halvag had said that many people were moving to be closer to the capital. I could understand why.

Aslaug did not allow us to stop in any of the towns, so we reached Dalsfjor by early afternoon. It was a fortified city on the shore of a fjord. The harbor was filled with ships of all sizes, from tiny fishing vessels to vast knarrs and spice ships. A black stone wall framing the city was guarded by archers who stood with their bows nocked and ready. The city was built onto the slope of a mountain. The houses were made from multi-colored stone that glittered like scales in the sun. The streets were paved with small white pebbles that looked like sea shells. At the highest point of the city stood the biggest longhouse I'd ever seen. It appeared to have been made from entire trees rolled and stacked to create a structure that loomed over the rest of the city. It had silver doors that gleamed like eyes.

We paused at the gate, but the guards knew Aslaug and let us pass without questions. Most of the inhabitants, clearly used to foreigners, ignored us, but a few children stood in the doorways of their houses. They pointed at Ersel's bright hair until she tugged her hood over her head to cover it.

Merchant carts bearing meat, fish, and strange fruits wheeled by us, as did farmers leading sheep and foals. A man leading a full-sized gray wolf passed, making Aslaug's stallion shy. He held two black wolf puppies against his chest. All around us were the sounds of people: the hammer of the blacksmith's forge, the steady chop of a butcher's axe, laughter, bargaining, and hoofbeats.

I'd only been to a city a handful of times. On occasion, I'd been allowed to travel with Mama when she brought our horses to market at Jorvik. I remembered the metropolis' high stone towers, the cathedral bells summoning worshippers of the new religion, and the muddy brown river that wound through the lower quarters. Lured by the promise of wealth, people of many cultures had lived together there.

The horse market in Jorvik had been a wonder. Every size, shape, and breed of equine had been for sale, tied up in makeshift stalls for inspection. Mama's warhorses had been some of the most coveted, and people had lined up all day to watch the auctions. My heart had swelled with pride when I led our foals into the ring. I wondered what the market here would be like. My gaze followed the gray wolf until she and her owner disappeared into the crowd.

Aslaug didn't let us stop to gawk. They led us straight through the city toward the longhouse. The steep incline of the road soon stole the ponies' breath. I doubted they were used to carrying riders. By the time we reached the garden at the top of the mountain, they were lathered, as was Ersel, from nudging her reluctant mount forward. Aslaug's mare still looked immaculate; her dark coat gleamed like polished obsidian, and she carried her head proudly, as if she knew how beautiful she was. I sank lower in my saddle; a flush warmed my cheeks. This pony was, at best, a mount for a child. What would the jarl think of me?

Up close, the longhouse was even more impressive. The silver gates were inlaid with precious stones and sea pearls. The walls were made from a type of tree I'd never seen before, with deep, jewel-red bark. Smaller houses for servants and visitors surrounded it. I could hear laughter and clashing swords coming from the rear of the house. At least some of the jarl's warriors must be here practicing. After the lack of training I'd seen from Haakon's mercenaries, it was encouraging to know this ally might have trained, career warriors at his disposal.

I slowly dismounted. In such a short time, I'd already started to lose riding fitness. My knees ached from the long ride and the little beast's width. Fjara had been much narrower, with a more flowing gait than the pony's choppy strides. A stable boy dressed in the jarl's livery took my reins, then helped Ersel dismount.

Aslaug jumped down, but kept hold of their reins. They whispered something to the boy, but I couldn't make out the words.

"The jarl is expecting you," they said to me. "You can go in. I will take your crew to a guesthouse. We'll bring food for them, and you can eat when you have finished with the jarl. You are welcome here as long as you wish to stay."

I nodded, even though my mouth suddenly felt dry with apprehension. I didn't like the idea of going into the feasting hall alone or leaving Ersel behind with my crew. But Aslaug had seen Ersel's power. I doubted they would let me take her into my meeting. My hand clenched at my side, but I stepped forward and fixed Aslaug with a wooden smile.

"Lead on," I said. If the jarl was willing to give us a whole house, then he must not have thought of me as a silly girl with no experience. We were meeting as equals. I tried to hold on to that thought as Aslaug knocked on the metal door.

The doors swung open, revealing a long, dim hall. Aslaug gestured for me to step inside. I took a deep breath, straightened my back, and walked across the threshold. The doors closed behind me.

Flickering beeswax candles lined the walls, but there were no obvious windows. The main chamber was the biggest hall I'd ever seen, with no doors to other rooms. Rugs dyed in orchid, cerulean, and deep green covered the floor. Tapestries depicting gruesome naval battles hung between the candles on the wall. The warm air smelled of sandalwood. This jarl had wealth and connections with merchants in the East and he wanted me to know it. I set my jaw and forced myself to look straight ahead. I wasn't a peasant. I wasn't going to gawk at the lord's finery. I was a stryimaðr and I needed to act like it.

A lone figure sat at the end of the hall on a throne on a raised platform. There were no guards or servants. I would have the jarl's full attention as I made my case. Unable to see the jarl clearly, I squinted in the low light. Then my eyes widened. No one had mentioned that the jarl was a woman. Female jarls were as rare as pearls.

Jarl Honor reclined on a high-backed wooden throne with her legs crossed primly at the ankles. Her skin was deep brown, and she wore her long, black hair in tight braids. She had high, noble cheekbones and bright green eyes. Her lips were quirked in a half smile. A sable mantle was wrapped around her shoulders. Gold rings adorned each of her slender fingers. She was beautiful, commanding, and regal—everything I wanted to be. I knelt on the dais before her. She extended her hand for me to kiss her rings, then lifted a bejeweled goblet to her lips.

"My húskarl tells me that you have come to ask for our support in retaking the Kjorseyrr coast, specifically the township now held by the late Jarl Haakon's men," she said.

"Yes. They hold children from my town as prisoners."

The jarl studied me. She rested the goblet on a little wooden table beside the throne. "And why should my thegns and I care about this?"

My mouth fell open. Of all the reactions I'd been playing out in my mind, that I might be met with blatant apathy hadn't occurred to me. I could picture Yarra so clearly, sitting atop Mjolnir and laughing with Lief beside her. The jarl couldn't be so heartless as to ignore their fate.

"Why should you care about children being held prisoner?" I ground out. "They're innocent. You would see them be butchered when they come of age?"

"Many people in the world are innocent."

"They're my people." I dug the tip of my hook into my thigh to keep myself in check. "And my grandmother was born in one of your villages. My kinsman, Halvag, lives there still. These children are kin to your own people."

Jarl Honor was silent. I struggled not to fidget, but when her gaze rested on my hook, I said defensively, "I fight just as well as before. Maybe better."

"I don't doubt it. You carry yourself like a warrior." Honor lifted the goblet and sipped her wine. "But since you landed on our shores, I have had eyes on you. What kind of jarl would I be if I just let a foreigner land on my coast with a hoard of fighting men? The old woman you met in the woods reports to me. She told me what I needed to know about you."

I bit the inside of my cheek. That encounter was shameful. But I had thought it would be a private shame, not something that would reach Honor's ears. I should have known better than to think that we could pass truly unseen. I had not disciplined the crew for their actions, and she probably thought I condoned them. I would fix that later.

Honor smiled, and wrinkles formed around her eyes. "She did say that you moved with incredible speed. Inala used to be a warrior, before she dedicated herself to Rán and chose a hermit's life close to the sea. She also saw a glimpse of the moving tattoos on your arms. Aslaug confirmed them."

"Then you know I could be an asset to you!" I exclaimed and held out my arms for her to inspect the markings. "Help me to free my town, and we'll all swear fealty to you. You could extend your reach across the sea. I would pay you tribute, govern for you."

She sighed. "And what kind of governor would you be? Inala says you do not trust your men and she could see that they have no love for you."

The fragile leash I had on my temper snapped. "You don't know anything about those men or what their ilk did to my town. My home is in ashes. You don't know what they took from me."

I braced myself, sure that she would order me to leave.

Instead, Honor set her jaw and leaned back on her throne. "You're wrong. I do care about Kjorseyrr. Those children are the last of a god's bloodline, the only navigators left. I am a religious woman, Ragna. I believe that slaying children of a god is sacrilege. We sailed to Brytten when we heard of Jarl Haakon's death. But I wanted to hear what you would say and see if you were different than the reports have told me. I cannot risk my own warriors to fight alongside men who may stab us in the back at any moment."

My head felt light. "You've been to Kjorseyrr?" I stammered.

"Even if none of those children show the marks now, their children might someday." The jarl looked down at her lap and twisted one of her rings. "As I said, I am religious. I also know what those children could bring to this land. We are rebuilding, but, as you have seen, many of our towns are still poor."

"You would have taken them?" I demanded. "You would have made them your slaves?"

The jarl's eyes flashed. "Never. We would have given them the choice. To come with us and join us as citizens or remain behind. They would be free here, and we would pray that, in time, they would choose to repay us—as Heimdallr himself chose when he favored Jarl Sigrid."

Jarl Sigrid? I had heard her name in our histories, but never of any association with the gods. My nose wrinkled, and I stowed the name away to ask questions later. "I could find you all the gold you need if you help me."

Honor shook her head; heavy braids fell across her face. "As I said, I am a religious woman. I know my history. Haakon, for all his other faults, was the same. It is not gold we want you to find."

A flush crept up my neck. Since the day I was taken captive, I had wondered what Haakon needed us to find. He had been one of the richest men in the world already, with no compunction about murdering and pillaging to get what he wanted. Honor knew why we had been attacked. She knew why I'd been taken and something about the history of my connection to Heimdallr. But if I betrayed my ignorance now, I might lose my chance to bargain.

"Why didn't you succeed?" I asked instead. "You may be rebuilding your provinces, but this city is enormous. You must have five hundred warriors at your disposal."

"The men stationed at Kjorseyrr have done more than recruit new warriors to their cause. They have a creature in their service who guards the prisoners."

"A creature?" My legs, already exhausted from the ride, were starting to go numb from kneeling. "What sort of creature?"

"An eight-legged horse that feeds on humans," Jarl Honor whispered. She gripped the carved snakes that wound over the arms of her throne. "A creature of Loki. The Trickster has their own stake in this and they will protect it. My warriors are fearful of the Trickster god. As they should be."

I thought back to the storm that had wrecked our ship. Ersel had been certain that the cyan waves and rough winds had been caused by Loki. Still, any admission of ignorance on my part was as good as admitting to the jarl that I was unprepared. I waited and said nothing.

The jarl stood and rested her hand on my shoulder. "Together, there is a chance we might defeat it. You know the island. You have a shapeshifter with you, who invokes Loki for her power. But I won't risk my thegns in battle with an incompetent leader we can't trust. Prove that you can lead your own crew—that you can make them respect you, care for your survival, and not just fear your immediate wrath—and we will sail together."

"How can I possibly make them do that?" I climbed to my feet on stiff legs to look her in the eyes. Permission be damned! "They hate me because I am a woman and young. I must be cruel to them, or they try to rise against me. They think I'm weak."

To my horror, Jarl Honor tossed her head back and laughed. "I'm a woman and I rule a province. Do you think it was easy for me when I first took power here? I prove myself daily, and yet I have reorganized this city according to my own beliefs. Let's take a walk."

Still fuming, I followed the jarl out of the longhouse to a field with archery targets and fenced dueling rings. Warriors of many genders fought with wooden practice swords, aimed bows, or brushed beautiful, muscled horses. The animals had clear, alert eyes and crested necks. I'd ridden to meet the jarl aboard a fat cart pony. No wonder she wasn't taking me seriously.

Grizzled veterans with white beards helped novices tighten girths and nock arrows. Conversation and laughter filled the space. I bit my lip and stuck close to the jarl. Had I ever heard my crew sound so at ease? Sometimes, when I was practicing below deck or with Ersel, I had heard them playing cards or laughing beneath the stars. But they'd always stopped when I had opened the hatch.

Honor gazed at the practice yard, where her warriors sparred. "My mother was a black merchant sailor from the South who fell in love with a white thegn. I was born in this city, and yet, for years, because of the color of my skin, people here saw me as foreign. I have struggled for everything that I have against people who wanted to see me fail."

She clapped her hands twice. The warriors immediately stopped their activity, dropped their weapons, and knelt on the grass. Honor took my arm and strode into the middle of the yard. The thegns watched her from their knees, perfectly still, but their smiles had not vanished.

A woman with white hair and a scar across her cheek rose and brought one of the horses to the jarl. He was a striking animal, dapple-gray with a proud, deep neck. His coat was polished to a sheen. "He's just four," the warrior said, unable to keep the excitement from her voice. She nodded toward a heavyset black man with a thick beard. "Fjarin says he is the best of the yield. We will have him trained for you."

"Thank you, Mjoll," Honor said. "He is a credit to you. I will ride him proudly."

The woman flushed and murmured her thanks.

Jarl Honor took the reins and stroked the animal's neck. She smiled at her warriors. "Please, do not let us interrupt you."

Some of the warriors resumed their practice, but many others hovered around us, waiting for their chance to speak to the jarl.

"They adore you," I whispered. On our voyage, I had relied on fear to keep control of my men. It had never occurred to me that there might be another way to command my crew's respect. Still, these thegns had pledged themselves to Honor alone. They were honorable, principled warriors, nothing like the cut-throat mercenaries who followed me.

Honor nodded. "When you can say the same for the crew you lead, come back to speak with me. Until then, I'm afraid we cannot help you."

*   *   *

I LEFT JARL HONOR TO address her thegns. The stable boy who had taken my pony waited for me in the courtyard, where he pruned winter roses with a long pair of bronze sheers. He rushed over when I approached. "We've laid a meal for you and your crew in the Blue House, styrimaðr. The jarl apologizes that she cannot dine with you today, but I assure you that you will be very comfortable. If you'll follow me?"

The boy led me to a building made entirely of shimmering blue gemstones and white seashells. In the sun, it glittered like a pendant. I smiled. When I'd pictured Ersel's home under the ocean, I'd always imagined something like this. I knew she had lived under an iceberg, but still, I hoped she would feel at home here.

I pushed open the door. The main room had two long tables with benches dominating the space. Fur and pelts for sleeping were rolled up against the walls. An open door at the rear of the room led to a bedchamber with a four-poster bed. The jarl's servants had spread a feast on the tables. My crew was clustered on the benches. They gorged themselves on fresh blackberries and crusty bread smothered with butter. There was a suckling pig on the first table, still uncarved. A steward stood behind it with knives at the ready.

Ersel and Trygve sat together at the second table, but there was no room beside them. Ersel gave me an apologetic shrug when she caught my eye, but she'd barely spoken to me on the ride. Maybe I had overstepped by demanding that she transform in our meeting with Aslaug. I would have to apologize later.

I took a seat next to Smyain instead. He didn't notice me when I sat down. He gobbled down a slice of bread, crumbs collecting in his beard, then reached for another. When I cleared my throat, he started and dropped the bread onto his plate.

"Apologies, styrimaðr," he murmured. "We should have waited for you."

I held back a tart reply. If I wanted Jarl Honor's assistance, I had to make this crew accept me, *like* me. I would have to bury whatever hostility I felt for now—even if I was still annoyed with him for flirting with Ersel and making us fight over the pinecone. I fixed him with a wide smile. "There was no way you could have known how long I'd be. Please, eat. You must be famished."

His brow furrowed, but he didn't need to be given permission twice. He reached for a handful of berries and stuffed them into his mouth.

"Shall we cut the meat, my lady?" one of the stewards called to me.

Through a mouthful of bread, Torstein shouted, "She isn't a lady. She's a styrimaðr."

A genuine smile pulled at my lips before I bit it back. I could play the part of a more benevolent captain to win Honor's favor, but I couldn't start believing it myself. As soon as I started to believe my men cared for me, I'd be in danger.

"Cut the meat!" I banged my bronze cup on the table. "And bring me some ale."

While the steward carved the pig and distributed slices, I turned my attention to Smyain. Starting table conversation had never come easily to me, so I cleared my throat again to get his attention. Smyain had been about to take a drink from his tankard, but he put it down when he heard me.

"Yes?" he asked, instantly attentive in a way I'd never noticed or appreciated. "Do you need me to do something?"

I shook my head. "No, I just… I'm curious about you. I haven't really spoken with you, or any of the men for that matter."

We had sailed together for weeks, but I realized, with a touch of unexpected shame, that the sum of our conversations had been barked orders. As their captain, I should know something about them, if only to manipulate them better.

He started at me, wide-eyed, and a morsel of cheese fell from his lips. "About me?"

"Yes," I pressed on. "Tell me. How did you come to be in Jarl Haakon's service?"

He scowled and ground his teeth. I worried that I'd chosen the wrong question. But after a pause, he said, "I didn't really have much choice. I'm from a farming village in the mountains near Leirag. My mother was alone with six children, and I was the third, so when I came of age, I was just a burden—wouldn't inherit the family farm. I was too old to be taking food out of the mouths of the little ones." He shrugged. "Haakon went through men like old socks. He used us and wore us out with as much regard. But it meant there was always a place at the jarl's manor for a young man to try his luck. I arrived in Bjornstad and was out on a ship within the week."

"With no training? Straight from a farm?" I'd spent years training with my weapons for a hope of being good enough to join a jarl's household. Even then, if the jarl had accepted me, I had expected to spend years more under the tutelage of a more experienced warrior before I'd be sent on an expedition. Fighters who sailed under a jarl's colors, even mercenaries, usually spent years as apprentices to a thegn. Aslaug and the two men who had come with them rode as if born to a horse and carried their weapons as extensions of their bodies. That kind of movement took years to learn. I had never thought that my men possessed that level of skill—most of them had never advanced in rank—but to hear that Haakon had sent Smyain to fight with no training at all…

Smyain grimaced. "If we survived a few raids, then maybe the jarl would take an interest. Men like Torstein who rose to styrimaðr had some training. I was never good enough to merit interest. The one time I met the jarl, he said I was like a cockroach—not fancy, no style, but I just kept surviving."

Smyain had a full, yellow beard, but beneath it his skin was still youthful. He couldn't have been older than his early twenties. How long had he been fighting untrained? Just hoping to survive? I didn't want to feel sorry for him, but this wasn't a life he had chosen.

"And did you ever go on a raiding mission?" I asked hesitantly.

He shook his head. "My captain was assigned to protect merchant vessels. We sailed out as far as the coast of Groenwald and would watch for pirates and looters trying to take what belonged to the jarl. For conquering new lands... Haakon sent better fighters than me." He gave me an apologetic smile. "Not exactly selling myself, am I?"

His confession shouldn't have given me confidence. If the men I led now were all untrained like him, recruited as sword-fodder by Haakon, then we didn't stand a chance against his more-seasoned fighters. Still, part of me felt more at ease after hearing his story. He had not been a raider, burning homes and terrorizing innocent people. He was a farmer who had found himself at sea just trying to stay alive.

The steward carefully placed a choice cut of pork in front of me. He filled my tankard to the brim with frothy cider. I took a sip. It was tart and strong, just the way I liked it. I stabbed the pork with my knife. It was so tender that it broke away with a flick of my wrist. That made me smile. Cutting meat precisely was something I still struggled to do with one hand.

When I had finished eating, I rose from my bench and sought out Ersel. Purple berry juice stained her mouth and hands, so I knew she had eaten, but her face had a sickly pallor, and there were dark shadows under her eyes.

"Are you all right?" I asked.

"Just a bit tired, I think." She pointed to the bedroom at the back of the house. "I assume we'll take that? I think I should lie down for a while."

After my relative success in talking to Smyain, I had planned to spend more time talking with the men before retiring, but after the way I'd displayed her to Aslaug, I decided to go with her. I took her arm to steady her as we walked to the bedroom. The crew hardly paid us any attention. Most of the men were still stuffing whatever food remained into their mouths and getting drunk on Jarl Honor's seemingly endless supply of ale. Suckling pigs were expensive, as was drink. If I couldn't prove myself to her, and quickly, I wondered how long the jarl's hospitality would last.

I closed the doors behind us. Ersel sank bonelessly onto the bed. I cursed myself for not realizing how much riding would tire her out. I was only a few weeks out of practice and my legs still ached from such a long journey. When we travelled back to the coast, I would see if there was a wagon she could ride in.

A bucket filled with soapy water stood beside the bed. Someone had left two new sets of clothes for us, draped over the chair by the window: identical pairs of cream trousers, pale blue tunics, and gray cloaks that fastened with blue glass pins. It would be wonderful to change clothes at last. I knelt beside the bucket and hastily scrubbed my arms and neck. The water was tepid, but it smelled of lilac and rose petals. I would have loved a full bath, but I wouldn't complain to our host. My hair was matted from the ocean gales, and salt grains clung to my scalp. I leaned back into the bucket and submerged as much of my hair as possible.

After washing, I flopped down beside Ersel and stared up at the ceiling.

"I'm sorry," I said.

"For?"

"Making you shift in front of Aslaug." The more I thought about it, the more I realized what a violation it had been. I hadn't asked her, and her clothes had torn. I'd displayed her like a prize. I looked down at my lap, disgusted with myself.

Ersel pinched the bridge of her nose. "I know you didn't mean anything by it. And it's not as though I haven't shifted in front of humans. But I didn't leave my home and come with you to be treated like this. I'm not a weapon. I'm here because I want to see the world and because I care for you, but if you treat me like a member of your crew whom you can order about, I'll go."

"I should have asked. Before, when we were alone. I can tell it's been bothering you."

"I felt naked," she said, her voice quivering. "For the first time."

"I'm sorry."

She scooted closer to me and propped herself up weakly on one elbow. "So, will Jarl Honor help?"

I let out an aggravated sigh. "Not yet. She says that my men lack discipline and don't follow me out of any real loyalty. She says she won't risk her own thegns to sail with a crew like that."

Ersel ran her hand over the bed's ornately carved headboard. "Look at this place. They have everything. She's just making excuses. She could take your town back by herself if she wanted to."

"She tried." I cast a furtive glance at the door, then dropped my voice to a whisper. "There's more guarding the town than you saw."

"What?"

"There's a creature. The jarl said it belongs to Loki. It guards the keep where they're holding the children. Honor has been on the island. She's seen it herself. The only reason she'd even talk to me about going back is because of my magic and because you're with me and you know Loki."

Ersel eased herself up on the pillows. "I don't think anyone really knows Loki. I want nothing else to do with them."

"I won't make you fight them," I said. "I won't even ask you to. I just need you to tell the jarl whatever you know of them."

"You can't fight whatever Loki will send. The only way to beat them is to play their game and win. I sailed with you to get away from them, not to go through this again. I'm done with Loki and their tricks and with other people trying to control me. If you care for me, keep me out this." She rolled over, her back to me.

I blew out the candle on the bedside table. I wouldn't ask her to fight, but she would come around when the time came. I knew she would. Part of her had to want revenge on Loki for what they'd done to her. If she thought we could beat the god, really beat them, then she would want to play a part in that. Wouldn't she?

Cyan lamplight pooled into the room, coming from the window. I jumped out of bed and wrenched the window open, hoping to catch the eavesdropper. I didn't want my men knowing that a creature of Loki waited for them or that the jarl wasn't satisfied with my leadership. But when I looked out into the night, there was nothing. I could only see the black shadows of the jarl's fruit trees and the orange fire-glow from the city below the hill.

I closed the shutters and crept to the bed. Ersel was already snoring, but her skin was cold to the touch. I pulled the thick wool blanket over her shoulders and smoothed her sweaty hair off her face. One of the sea pearls came loose in my hand. I cupped it in my palm and stared down at it. It had a faint pink sheen and was oblong rather than round. Not a perfect specimen, but it might still buy a horse. Ersel's hair draped over the pillow. The pearl closest to her temple was an exact sphere and soft, milky white. I hesitated for only a moment before gently teasing it from her hair. I tucked both pearls into the pouch at my belt. She would never miss them.

I lay down and tried to sleep, but my eyes kept travelling to the closed window. I couldn't shake the feeling that someone had been listening.

I LAY AWAKE FOR MOST of the night, listening to Ersel's quiet snoring. By morning, I had a plan to win my men's loyalty. Smyain had never received any weapons training, and many of the others were probably in the same position. How I could I expect them to follow me willingly when they didn't have the skills to the fight the enemies I led them toward? Wherever their lives took them after we took back Kjorseyrr and parted ways, those skills would pay. If I taught them, they would be grateful to me.

Ersel still had not recovered from the ride. She woke damp with sweat. A few of her mermaid's scales had erupted through the magic binding her to human form. They dotted her cheeks like flecks of silver dust. I left her to rest and went in search of Aslaug.

I was certain that my plan had merit, but if I was going to train with my men, we would need better weapons, targets, and horses. I'd never seen most of them ride. I didn't know if they could swing an axe or a sword from the saddle. If Smyain's story was typical, some might not even be able to shoot a bow.

I found my crew sprawled out on the floor of the guesthouse's main chamber. Some had unrolled their furs and made beds, but many others had fallen asleep where they'd sat at the table. Trygve was asleep with his head on a plate; meat drippings stuck to his beard. I walked up behind him and cleared my throat. He jerked to attention, hands splaying, and sent his ale tankard flying. I rolled my eyes as he sputtered apologies.

"I'm going to find the húskarl." I grabbed a wooden cup and carefully poured him some water from the jug. "Make sure none of them leave here before I get back."

Trygve rubbed at his eyes. "Okay."

"Don't fall back to sleep," I cautioned. "And check on Ersel. She's ill."

He sipped his water slowly. "Should we send for a healer?"

"Do you think a healer would know what to make of her?" I shook my head. "I think she's just tired from the ride. She's not used to walking as a human yet, much less riding for a full day."

I turned to the door, but Smyain waved his hand at me. He groaned and climbed to his feet. "Do you need someone to go with you?" he asked. "We don't know the people here. They might not all be as friendly as the jarl."

"I'd feel better if you weren't completely alone," Trygve said.

Smyain dusted off his tunic and shot me a grin. "I'm a survivor, remember? I'll make myself useful."

His volunteering was unexpected, but they were right. I would be safer with company. I nodded, and Smyain followed me outside. It was a bright morning, but frost still clung to the trees. Frozen leaves crunched under our boots. The city below was quiet, and the streets were empty. I figured that being the húskarl, Aslaug would have a house somewhere on the jarl's hill, so I set off across the courtyard.

We passed the jarl's stable. The sweet, musty scent of horses and hay was so much like home that it lured me inside. A low nicker greeted us, and I blinked back homesick tears. The pony I'd ridden yesterday had the stall nearest the entrance, and when he saw me his little ears pricked straight up. He whinnied again.

I went to him and stroked the whorl of hair at the center of his forehead. "You're no war steed," I said.

"No," Smyain said behind me. I could hear the smile in his voice. He stepped closer and held out a handful of frozen blackberries to the pony. "But he would try for you. Wouldn't you, lad?"

The pony nibbled the edge of my hook. I leaned over his stall door to scratch his withers with the point, as I had done before. He stretched his neck to the side to give me better access, and his eyes rolled back in his head. I laughed. I never would have expected my hook to make such a good horse scratcher, but the little beast seemed to love it.

We walked down the aisles of stalls. My gaze rested on an obsidian mare with a jagged white star. She reminded me of Fjara, with her dark coat and delicate concave muzzle. I patted her neck. Her coat was impossibly soft. Someone must have spent hours every day brushing her. Her eyes had a rim of white around the iris, which gave her a curious expression. I swallowed a sob. In this stable, I was home again—up early in the morning, talking to Fjara before Mama woke up and put me to work cleaning stalls or mixing grain. It was how almost every day of my childhood had begun.

I slipped into the stable beside the mare and ran my hand across her back. She had a slight sway to her spine and one of her rear pasterns was too upright. If she had been one of our foals, Mama would have put special shoes on her as a filly to correct her stance. By now, she would stand straight.

"My mother bred horses like these," I said, not sure if I was talking to the mare or Smyain, or why I was sharing at all. "People came from all over the island to see them."

Smyain offered the mare a few blackberries. She took them delicately, barely brushing his palm with her lips, like a queen accepting a jewel. "I only rode a carthorse before I entered the jarl's service." His hazel eyes swept over my face. "You must miss them."

The pity in his voice snapped me out of the memory. I didn't want that from him or anyone on the crew. I straightened and gave the mare a final pat. "We should go."

He scuffed his foot on the ground, looking as if he might say something else. But then he shrugged and waved goodbye to the mare, as if she were a small child instead of a warhorse.

As we approached the barn door, it swung it open. Aslaug stood in the entrance, wearing wintergreen trousers, a gold tunic that swept past their knees, and a long, black cloak trimmed in flame-colored fox fur. Their fine attire marked their high status in the city. They folded their arms over their chest; their expression was wary. "What are you doing in here? Not leaving?"

"No." I rolled my eyes. "We're not here to steal a horse and run. I didn't come all this way for that. We were looking for you and got sidetracked."

Aslaug's face softened. They walked to the obsidian mare and extended their hand for her to stiff. "Beautiful, isn't she? She's one of the jarl's favorites."

"Her back is a bit swayed, and her pasterns are too upright," I said. "You should put special shoes on her. It should have been done when she was a foal, but it might not be too late."

Aslaug glanced down the horse's legs. "I don't see it," they said. "But I didn't grow up with horses. Even here, we've heard of your mother's stock. What did you need me for?"

"I need equipment. The jarl wants us to train. If we're to do that, we'll need a place to practice, some targets, and suitable mounts."

Aslaug's eyebrows shot up, but if they knew what the jarl had truly said in our meeting, they kept it to themself. "That's easy enough to arrange. There's a field farther up the hill where we graze the sheep in the summer. I can have some targets brought up for you, and bows. We don't have many horses to spare, but I can let you use a few of our older mounts. They don't see combat anymore, but they know their job."

Part of me had hoped for something flashy, but if the crew didn't know how to maintain paces or match strides, it was probably best they start on horses that were easy.

"I will offer my assistance, as well," the húskarl said. "When the jarl can spare me. I know a few things about weapons."

"Thank you," I said and gave Smyain a small push toward the door. The húskarl had probably only offered so they could keep a closer eye on me and make sure we didn't try to steal any of the horses they loaned us, but Aslaug's help would almost certainly be better than the training I could provide. "We will gather the crew and meet you in the field."

*   *   *

WE SPENT THE WHOLE MORNING training on the field Aslaug had prepared. I was pleased to find that, although most of my crew came from farming or trading backgrounds, most were proficient with an axe, hammer, and sword. The men sparred as I watched them with a critical eye. Their style wasn't graceful, but they knew where to strike. Aslaug walked among the pairs correcting stances and grips with infinite, gentle patience. They never raised their voice or became frustrated when a man failed to understand a new maneuver. It was easy to see why the jarl relied on them so heavily.

Riding and archery were another story. Even Torstein sat ahorse like a sack of rocks and managed to hit the target only once with an arrow. The men had grumbled on the beach about being forced to walk inland, but I was starting to suspect that had all been for show. I was grateful to the solid, old horses who never put a foot wrong or bucked, even when the riders jerked their mouths. Riding was my domain. I'd never ridden as well as Yarra, but Mama had taught me everything she knew. I had grown up caring for warhorses. While Aslaug continued to help with melee, I barked instructions to the riders.

"I've seen young children ride better than you!" I shouted at Torstein when he missed the target for the third pass. His roan gelding pinned back its ears. It wasn't exactly a fair comment, as Yarra was a better rider than I was, too, but I wouldn't admit that.

He pulled up beside me and tossed his sword on the ground. "Aye," he said. "Better I stick to ships. Riding into a fight is more you islanders' way."

"If the stories about your wreck are to be believed, you're not very good with ships either."

I expected to see anger on his face, but he laughed. He swung his leg over the gelding's back and hit the ground hard. "Probably not. But at least if I keep sailing to new places, I stay ahead of my reputation."

By the time the sun reached its full height, I was bone-weary. I clapped my hands to get the crew's attention, then dismissed them. They trotted off at once, racing each other in the direction of the guesthouse and lunch, tossing their weapons aside with little thought. I sighed and began collecting the discarded steel. I didn't want the jarl to think we were ungrateful. I'd need to teach the men better respect for their weapons.

"I'll see to that," Aslaug said. They held two axes in their hands already. "You look exhausted."

I flashed them a weary smile. Aslaug had been training all morning too—and had been moving more than me—but they still walked with light-footed grace, as if they had only just risen. My crew and I had a long way to go to match the húskarl's fitness. I gathered the horses' reins and led them back to their stable.

At the house, the crew sat on long benches. The tables were laden with a feast of chicken, apples, and assorted jams, but this time, no one had touched the food. They watched me enter with hungry eyes and kept their hands folded in their laps. I smiled and gestured for them to begin. They didn't have to be told twice.

A morning of exercise had sharpened their appetites. They had earned this meal.

Torstein and Steinair shifted on the bench to make a space for me, but Trygve and Ersel were not seated among them, and the bedroom door was closed. I shook my head. "I'm going to retire for a while. Make sure you save me something to eat."

In the bedroom, Trygve knelt at Ersel's side holding a bucket. She leaned over it and dry-heaved. A trail of bile dripped down her chin. I rushed to her. Her form had shifted; the human legs were gone, and the blanket hardly concealed her ever-moving tentacles. Topaz, lilac, and azure scales covered her body, but the webbing that usually grew between her fingers when she was in this form had not appeared. The blanket was wet with her sweat. I pulled it back and gasped. In her kraken's form, she normally had eight tentacles, but now there were only four. Was she stuck in the middle of a transition? Had her illness caused this?

"What hurts? What can I do?" I asked.

She opened her mouth to respond, then retched into Trygve's bucket again.

"We need to get a healer," Trgyve said grimly. "I know they might not have seen anything like her, but she can't even keep water down."

I scrambled to my feet and pushed open the door to the main chamber. "Fetch a healer!" I demanded.

The crew turned on their benches to stare at me, mouths full. When none of them rose, my eyes narrowed. We'd had a good day practicing on the hills, but allowing them to become more comfortable with me was a mistake if it meant they couldn't follow orders.

"Now!" I growled. My change in tone had all of them on their feet and out of the house in an instant.

I went back to the bedroom and sat on the bed. Ersel's tentacles had vanished completely, replaced by her mermaid's tail. As I watched, her body convulsed, and her scales vanished. The tail remained, but with its bare, sensitive, pink skin exposed. Ersel let out a chilling scream before she shifted back into a human girl.

"I don't think she can control it," Trygve said. "Maybe the healer will let some of her blood to get the infection out."

I clasped Ersel's clammy hand. Her eyes were focused on the headboard. I wasn't sure she was aware I was here. How had this happened? Of all of us, she had eaten the best on the journey. She'd never suffered from illness at sea, and we hadn't come close to anyone sick on shore.

She convulsed again, and three tentacles grew alongside her human legs.

The healer wouldn't be able to help her. I knew that. From the way she was moving between forms, losing control of her abilities… there had to be a disease in her magic. The only being who could help her was the one who had given that power to her.

"We need to pray to Loki," I said.

"No!" Ersel wheezed. She attempted to sit up, then fell back on her pillows. Her bloodshot eyes locked on mine. "I never want to see them again. I told you that. Promise me."

"Shh, I won't." I stroked her hair while looking sharply at Trygve. Ersel's fear of the god was clouding her senses, just as before. I wasn't stupid enough to make a deal with Loki. But what could it hurt to pray to them? To bring them here? I didn't have to agree to their terms, and they might be able to save her.

They had followed us across the sea and tried to destroy us with a hurricane. I had believed that was all in pursuit of Ersel, but after what Jarl Honor had told me, I wasn't so sure. If they had their own stake in my homeland, in my navigator's marks, didn't I deserve to hear for myself how the god wanted to use me?

I drew Trygve into the corner of the room. "We need to summon them."

Trgyve shook his head. "They're a god. You can't just send one of the men to fetch them from the tavern."

"They'll come. They want something from me too."

"You said you wouldn't," Trygve said stubbornly. "You promised her."

"So what?" I hissed. "I let her die because she's scared? She doesn't know what she's saying. She's delirious. After everything she went through with Loki, she's still alive, isn't she? If they had wanted her dead, they're a god, I'm sure they could have found a way."

Trygve's shoulders slumped. "As you think best."

The bedroom door banged open and Torstein appeared, an elderly woman in tow. The healer was small and prim; her long gray hair was swept back into a utilitarian bun. She held a suede-covered equipment roll in her arms. I moved aside to let her sit by Ersel. She shook her head and did not move from the doorway.

"What is she?"

Ersel's body convulsed and shifted fully into her mermaid's form. The healer screamed. "What is she?" the old woman repeated and glared at Torstein. "I was told to come treat one of the jarl's guests who had taken ill with fever. I assumed she would be human. Not some kind of god-spawn."

"She isn't god-spawn," I said and fought to keep my voice gentle, even though I wanted to grab the old woman and shake her. "She's a mermaid."

"Mermaids aren't real," the healer sniffed. She crept cautiously over and then gave me a pat on the arm. "If that's what it told you, then you've been deceived. Maybe it's one of Loki's beasts."

"She's not a creature of Loki," I snapped and rolled up my sleeves so she could see my moving tattoos. "The only one here who is god-spawn is me and I'm pretty sure the jarl knows about that."

"Just give her something for the fever." Trygve pointed to the roll in the healer's arms. "You must have something that will bring it down."

"Whatever she is, her constitution may not be like ours," the healer said. "Whatever I give her could be poisonous to her system. The jarl will throw me in the dungeons if I poison one of her guests. I'm sorry. I cannot treat her."

She clutched her roll and rushed for the door.

"What will she do to you if you let one die?" I screamed at her back, but the door slammed closed.

Torstein edged over to Ersel's bed. Her tentacles flashed, then changed color, each long limb a different hue of gray. "What's wrong with her?"

I closed my eyes. "If I knew, I wouldn't have sent you to fetch that old bitch."

"We think it's a disease in her magic," Trygve said. "Thank you for your assistance."

Torstein understood the dismissal. He shuffled to the door. His hand had closed on the knob before he said to me, "We'll keep her in our prayers, styrimaðr."

I was so shocked by his words that I said nothing as he left the room. Praying for her? They all hated her. And with magic she couldn't control, they should fear her more than ever. Ersel whimpered, and I took her hand. Their hatred of her was my fault. How many times had I used her to threaten them? She had been my weapon against them all along.

I ripped off a piece of the blanket and submerged it in the now-freezing bucket of water. I pressed it to Ersel's cheek. Her sickness was my fault too. I had taken her hundreds of miles from her home, with no regard for how it might affect her. She hadn't started eating human food until a few days ago. Maybe the healer was right—our food might be toxic to her, and it was the only thing I'd thought to offer her. I'd even ridiculed her the first night, when she had refused Halvag's porridge.

"Keep her cool and get her to drink if you can," I said. "I'm going for a walk."

Eleven

DESPITE MY TIRED LEGS, I trekked to the practice field. It was the only place I could think of to be alone. I'd left without my cloak, and the sharp wind made the hairs stand up on my arms. The field looked bigger and emptier without my men and when the dim winter light elongated all the shadows.

I knelt in the grass, thinking that Loki might respond better to an attempt at piety. Unlike Ersel, I was a vár child. The God of Lies had no innate affinity for children born in my season. Ersel was of haustr. The Trickster's changeable autumn nature was in her blood. The damp earth soaked through my trousers. I rested my hand and hook in my lap. At first, the markings didn't move, but when I brought my wrists together, the map stretched on my skin, showing a more detailed view of the city farther down the mountain.

I glanced at the purple dusk sky. I didn't have a lot of experience in praying to the gods. I'd prayed a few times at sea to Aegir or Ran, but that had been fear talking. Nobody in my family was very religious. Mama, certainly, had never prayed. *We were beyond the gods' reach,* she had told me, smoothing back my hair, when I'd asked why we never made offerings like the other families' in the town. *And they are no less flawed than we are.*

Even then, Mama had refused to tell me the whole story. Heimdallr had fallen in love with my ancestor and had left her, cursing both to a life of sadness and want. The gods were selfish, calculating beings. They would only help me if they thought I could offer them something. According to Mama, that was all I needed to know.

My stepfather had been more pious and had told us some of the gods' legends. He had kept a statue of Frigg in his workshop and had sometimes kissed it while he murmured his prayers. Of all the gods, I knew, Loki interacted most readily with humans. Sometimes they bestowed blessings—incalculable wealth and prestige—on the worthy. At other times, they played with their human supplicants, pitting them against each other and stirring the embers of conflicts that lasted for centuries. More than one war had begun because of the Trickster's meddling.

I whispered a prayer to the wind. Ersel thought of Loki as malice made divine. As I knelt in the field, I wondered which version of the god would come to me. Would the god bless me or curse me? Why had they trailed our ship?

I expected a grand entry. When Loki had first come to Ersel, they had appeared in the form of a sea turtle, then dramatically shapeshifted into a human. But instead of a magnificent appearance, the god just left me to wait. I knelt until my knees cramped, with only the sound of the wind and the distant murmur of the city for company. I sat, crossed my legs, and plucked absently at a blade of grass.

Maybe the jarl had been wrong. Maybe the Trickster had no stake in this at all, and their pursuit of our ship had been all about reclaiming the mermaid. Loki had tried to break Ersel, and she had beaten them. Impressed, they had offered her greater magic and a role as their agent. Ersel had refused, but she still bore their magic in the talisman she wore around her neck. Maybe the god simply could not bear the idea that they had lost to a mortal.

"What are you doing alone up here?" asked a child's voice. "It's late."

I turned to see a servant girl running toward me. She wore a faded green tunic with the jarl's sigil embroidered on the sleeve. It was so large for her that it hung past her knees. "Oh, I'm sorry. I thought you were someone else," she whispered.

"It's fine," I started to say, but her eyes had rested on my hook and the markings on my arms. I'd thought to display them, so the Trickster would know me, but now I was just cold and in no mood to be stared at. "Why are you here? Can't you see I'm praying?"

She cocked her head, blonde curls blowing everyway in the wind. "Praying for what?" She pointed to my markings with one of her slender fingers. "Is that a map?"

I clasped my arms behind my back, out of sight. "Don't you have work to be getting on with? I don't want to be disturbed."

She peered down at me with wide, unblinking green eyes. "I thought the whole point of coming here alone was that you were waiting to meet someone."

"What?" I demanded. But then I stopped and processed what the little girl had said. Her eyes brightened, the color intensifying every second until they matched the cyan waves that had tried to capsize my ship.

For a second, I contemplated prostrating myself at the god's feet. But Loki was already playing tricks on me, testing me. In all the stories, the people blessed by the Trickster had been strong and smart, worthy of a god's respect. If I wanted help, *real* help, I had to prove I was worth it too.

I stood and raised my eyebrow just a fraction. My heart beat wildly. "You took long enough."

Loki laughed in a child's high pitch. "I was busy with a believer in the city." They twirled around, letting me get a full look at them. "This girl, Aelin, died last night. She had the sweating sickness, as did her whole family, but she offered me her voice if I would help her brother to live. The boy will remain on the earth for now. I have a soft spot for the selfless."

I nodded, but I couldn't help wondering what they were insinuating with their words. I was far from selfless. I had ambitions and had done things I wasn't proud of to fulfill them. "Why not save the girl too," I asked, "if it was within your power to cure?"

"I have to get something out of it, don't I?" Loki asked, curling their legs and sitting on the ground. They patted the earth beside them. They wore a patronizing smile that did not belong on their child's face. "I have a soft spot for them because they are something I am not. They fascinate me. But my help never comes for free."

I reluctantly sat beside them. "Do you know why I called on you?"

"I expect it has something to do with your dying mermaid." Loki pointed down the hill toward the guesthouse. "We gods can be in more than one place at a time. Even now, I'm watching her through the window."

"What did you do to her?"

Loki sighed. "What's happening with Ersel has nothing to do with me. Whatever form she takes, she is a mermaid. Rán's children can't venture too far from the sea. The ocean is their lifeblood."

"Then how do I help her?" I asked, even though I thought I already knew the answer. If I wanted Ersel to live, I had to take her to the sea, maybe even all the way to her people. She was too sick to just abandon at the shore. And to do that, I might have to give up the chance to win Honor's allegiance and free Yarra. I wasn't sure I could make that choice.

Loki watched my face intently. "I might be able to help."

I braced myself. I had no intention of making a deal with them, but I did want to know what they thought I had to barter with. "What is it that you want?"

Loki looked down at their lap; full eyelashes swept down to curtain their emotions. Then the god's fingers brushed over their lips. A green mist erupted from their hand and washed the glamor of magic away. The girl's freckles and bright smile faded, replaced by Loki's own face. The god's eyes were that same shocking, unnatural cyan, and their cheeks were sharp like chiseled stone, but it was the threads binding their true lips that held my stare. Blood crusted the black string and open sores covered their mouth. I'd never imagined a god bleeding.

"To be heard," Loki said softly.

I swallowed. The sight of the strings binding their mouth was making me feel sick. What would I do to free myself from centuries of suffering? My amputated limb ached almost every day, and while I did not regret the decisions that had led to my injury, if someone offered me the chance to get rid of the pain, I would take it. "And you think I can help you with that?"

Jarl Honor had said that Loki's creature guarded the fortress where the children were being kept. I had told Haakon's men that the navigator's marks could show up at any time, and they had believed me. What bargain had those men already struck with the Trickster god? If there was something the god needed us to find, then it made sense for them to help guard Heimdallr's other descendants. But Loki was a god. They had to know what the warriors did not: that I was the only one still living in our generation who would ever bear the marks.

Loki nodded. "You are of Heimdallr's blood. His magic conceals pieces of a dagger that can break these ties. It's bloodbound magic. He'll never forgive me, but his kin can set things right."

"What do you mean?" I asked. The god moved closer to me. Their gaze focused on the exposed skin of my arms. Self-consciously, I crossed them over my chest.

"What do you know of your family's story?"

Admitting my ignorance was dangerous. Loki could spin my family's history however they chose. If they lied, I would be none the wiser. But Mama had taken the secret to her death, and I was tired of other people knowing more about my family—more about *me*—than I did.

"Not much," I whispered. "Only that the god Heimdallr had a child with my ancestor, a girl with red hair, and then left her."

"A girl?" Loki gave a delighted cackle. "If Sigrid could hear you, I'm sure she would have something to say about that."

"Sigrid?" It was the same name that Honor had mentioned. "The jarl?"

"She was at sea," the god said. "She was returning from a battle in the North that had claimed most of her most trusted thegns. A plague claimed the others. She was alone, ferrying their bodies back to their families when Heimdallr found her."

My eyes bulged. My ancestor had been a jarl. It seemed so outlandish that I struggled to believe it. And yet… if our ancestor really had been a simple peasant girl, why had Mama always shut down when I asked for more of the story? She had hated the idea of me following in my uncle's footsteps. How much more persistent might I have been, had I known my ancestor had been a such an acclaimed warrior?

"And they made love?"

"Worse. He *fell* in love with her." Some feeling—was it sadness?—tugged at their lips, causing the threads to tighten. "We gods do not control our own hearts. They belong to the Norns, mothers of fate. They gave Heimdallr's hjarta to Sigrid. So he accompanied her to her people. He lived with her, fought beside her. They had children together."

It seemed so cruel, for the mothers of fate to pledge a god to a mortal, whose years would be so short in comparison to his own. "And she died?"

Loki shook their head. "No. Heimdallr has a special place among the gods. It is his responsibility to guard Odin. When Asgard found him, Odin demanded that Heimdallr return."

I sucked in a sharp breath. "So he left her?"

Loki's eyes shone with a glassy brightness I couldn't quite read. "Yes," they said. "And Sigrid was a proud woman. After he left her and broke her heart, she wanted to make sure he couldn't return on a whim."

"And you helped her?"

"The Norns also pledged my heart in an... inconvenient fashion." Loki sighed and looked down. Then, as if suddenly noticing they still wore their child's attire, they snapped their fingers. A cloud of cyan enveloped them and they shifted into a lean, adult body to match their face.

"I hid Sigrid from Heimdallr, at her behest. But Heimdallr holds that against me." They traced fingers over the threads binding their lips. "When Odin bound me, he didn't intend for it to be forever. The only way I can cut these bonds is with a dagger, split in pieces across the world. Odin entrusted it to Heimdallr, who will never help me. You can find it."

"That's why you followed me." I stretched out my legs, seeking a more comfortable position now that my fear of the god was easing. "And you guard the children, because if I can't help you, maybe one of them can?"

"We both know none of them can." The Trickster rolled their eyes. "But in fifty years? A few of those children have the blood. Their descendants may bear the marks, so when the leader of Haakon's men called upon me and alerted me to their whereabouts, I was happy to make a deal with him. But I have been waiting a very long time already."

Loki reached for me and tilted my chin up to look them in the face. "You remind me of Sigrid. Not in the way you look, but your bearing. Your speech."

I flushed. Sigrid had commanded one god's love and another's respect. I dreamed of becoming a leader like that. "What was she like?"

"Fearless," Loki admitted. "Talented. She won many battles. Even against my own worshippers."

They cleared their throat. "So, you know what I want of you. And I know what you want of me. To save your mermaid friend, will you make a deal?"

I pulled away from them. Everything they said had the ring of truth to it, but it was so much to take in. Loki was the Trickster. There had to be an angle to what they were telling me, something I wasn't seeing. If I died, Loki would have to wait another generation for their salvation. But if I made a deal, I might be trapped by some impossible loophole in the god's wording, the way Ersel had been. I might spend my life enslaved to the god, never able to get to Yarra. A chasm of guilt opened inside me. Whatever we were to each other, I couldn't make that sacrifice.

"No. I won't make a deal with you. But if you help me now, I won't forget it."

"You would let her die?" Loki snapped. "I'm watching her now. Her breathing is getting shallower by the minute. I thought you cared about her."

"Why do you watch her? Is it all about me?" The god's eyes flickered to the grass, and I pressed on. "I think you still have plans for her. I don't think you'll let her die either."

"You think I care what happens to mortals? I've been alive for millennia. Ersel's entire lifetime is a moment for me."

"You gave her magic. You wanted her to come back to you." Part of me expected Loki to kill me where I sat for speaking to them like this, but I continued, voice trembling. "You're asking me if I can let her die. Can you?"

Loki started silently at me, nostrils flaring. Then they waved their hand, and, in a cyclone of cyan, both of us were transported to my room in the guesthouse. Trygve had fallen asleep in a chair by Ersel's bed.

"It'll break her heart, you know," Loki said as they sat on the bed. "When she realizes the god she hated was more willing to help her than the girl she loves."

I glanced down at Ersel's sleeping form. She had settled, for now, between her mermaid and her human form. She had a human body, but her scales covered her hands and feet. Would she ever forgive me for this? Would I forgive myself?

Whatever control I'd had over my emotions disappeared. "You think I want it to be this way?" I hissed at them, as angry tears forged hot trails down my cheeks. "You're making me choose between my home—my family—and her."

Leaning forward, Loki collected my tears on their finger. They brushed the tears across Ersel's lips. "Salt water," they explained while I stared at them. "A very temporary measure, but that should see us to the coast."

Their dismissal just made me cry harder. Ersel's scales receded, and a fraction of her color returned. I reached for her hand. She gripped my fingers as her eyes fluttered open.

Her gaze flitted to the god sitting beside her. She gave a resigned sigh and pulled her hand back. "You summoned them."

"There wasn't another choice," I said, clinging to the small hope that Loki wouldn't tell her there had been, that the god wouldn't tell her that I refused to make a deal to keep her safe. I had not been able to do what she had done for me, that day she saved me from being drowned by Havamal. The magnitude of my failure made me feel nauseous.

Ersel nodded. "What did you have to promise them?"

"I—"

"The deal is between us," Loki interrupted. They bent down and carefully scooped Ersel up in their arms.

"I'll find you once I'm recovered," she said.

Loki carried her through the window and into the night. I couldn't decide what I hoped. To see her again? To stop being too selfish to love her? Or that the god would take her far away, and she would never come back, so I would never have the chance to betray her again.

Part 2: The Navigator

And now my spirit bursts
from my chest,
my soul soars
over the whale-road
to all the reaches of the world.
It returns
eager and unsatisfied,
a wanderer screaming,
for the route unexplored.

—Adaptation of from *The Seafarer*

One

Ylir
Odin's Month
November

AFTER A FORTNIGHT IN DALSFJOR, the crew and I had settled into a routine. We rose at dawn and spent the early morning running laps around the field. We sparred with swords and axes until the afternoon, took our lunch, and then practiced mounted skills until the evening. By nightfall each day, most of the crew were too tired to even speak at dinner. I fell into my bed with dreamless exhaustion.

Daily, I noticed improvements. They sat straighter on the horses; their arrows consistently found their targets. And each day, Aslaug came to help us. The húskarl arrived first and left last, never complained, and approached each warrior with the same quiet patience, no matter how long it took them to learn. By now, I was sure that Jarl Honor knew what we were doing and had given Aslaug her approval.

With every lap we jogged together, or loose horse I tracked down, my relationship with my men started to improve as well. When we had set sail from Bjornstad months ago, I had acted the part of a commander, not quite believing in my own performance, scared that at any moment my crew would stop believing too. Now, command was starting to fit like a pair of new boots. It still pinched a little, but I was breaking it in, making it mine.

I structured our days to spend as little time in the guesthouse as possible. When I was alone in my bedroom, I noticed Ersel's absence the most. I thought about how she had laughed, and how it made it her eyes come alive. Then, I thought about her convulsing on the four-poster bed, and how I betrayed her. I trusted that Loki would bring her home, if only to hold it over me later. I was the only one in this generation who could lead Loki to the fragments of Heimdallr's dagger. Now that they were so close to their desire, I doubted the Trickster would want to wait until another navigator was born, even if they did send a creature to guard the rest of the bloodline.

I had told Aslaug and the jarl that Ersel had recovered enough to travel, but had decided to return to the sea until we sailed. I didn't mention Loki at all. *Ersel will meet us,* I'd insisted. She would watch the seas and find our ships once we sailed for Kjorseyrr. *The mermaids had a way of sensing the ships,* I'd lied over dinner with the jarl. *Ersel will be ready. We will not go unprepared against Loki.*

On the second Odinsdagr, Jarl Honor sought me out. I was sitting cross-legged on the wet grass, watching Steinair maneuver one of the horses around an obstacle course we'd constructed from firewood and bales of hay. The jarl wore a rich, burgundy dress, trimmed in white bear fur. Aslaug walked a reverent step behind her with a great wooden shield in their hands. I didn't miss the way the húskarl's eyes never strayed from the jarl as they walked.

I scrambled to my feet and tried to brush the wet grass off my trousers. I had been waiting for an invitation to dine with her again, to plead our case further and stress that my men were ready. Of course she would come to see us when my clothing was a mess and I hadn't prepared the crew. "Jarl! We weren't expecting you. I could have brought them down for you to inspect."

Honor smiled. "I wanted to see how you were getting on without something so formal as an inspection. Aslaug says it's been going well."

She kept walking, hugging the perimeter of the field. I trotted after her and glanced at Aslaug for an explanation. The húskarl pressed their lips together and turned their head. I scowled. I had come to think of Aslaug as an ally, but they were the jarl's thegn first.

When we had walked the full length of the field and the jarl had seen all the men at their practice, she turned to me. "They're coming along nicely. I have a test for you. Pass it and we will set sail next week."

Another test? She had said that winning my crew's loyalty was the test. Did this mean I had passed?

"Wasn't this the test?" I blurted.

"They do seem more at ease, and I am impressed by the work you're doing with them," said the jarl. "But commanding a practice field and fighting wooden targets is easy. I'm curious to see how they will react when they have to fight real enemies."

"Do you want to see us spar against your thegns?" I asked and instantly regretted the offer. Practice or not, if all the jarl's thegns moved like Aslaug, we didn't stand a chance. If she wanted us to attack one of the neighboring earldoms, I didn't like our odds either. With only twenty men, we would be restricted to unarmed hamlets. I wouldn't let her turn us into raiders.

"Oh, no," Honor said. "If our warriors are to work together, I don't want to set up artificial rivalries between them."

The jarl took my arm and walked me to the easternmost edge of the field. She pointed beyond the city walls to a barren, gray mountain half-hidden by clouds on the horizon. "There's a village about six miles from here, at the base of that mountain with the bald face. They've been reporting livestock missing at night and last week a child. I think there must be a wolf's den near it. Clear that out for me and report."

I had to bite my cheek to stop the gleeful laughter. She wanted us to hunt down a pack of wolves? Two archers could easily take down a pack. But if Honor thought this was a worthy test, I wasn't going to challenge her. The faster we got it done, the sooner we could set sail. I molded my face into neutrality and said, "Of course. Consider it done."

"I should say," the jarl said. "That the villagers have mentioned that the wolves are of abnormal size…"

How big could they be? At the market back home, I'd seen wolf pelts brought from the continent. They had been from creatures little bigger than dogs. In the north of Brytten, we had wolves the size of ponies with brilliant white fur like the coveted ice bears. Since I was twelve, I'd been sent to kill ice wolves that raided the town sheep flocks. With twenty men, this pack wouldn't stand a chance.

"Of course," I said again. "We'll leave at once."

The jarl smiled and motioned to Aslaug. The húskarl held out the wooden shield they had been carrying. "A gift," they said.

"The jarl had it made for you. We hope it will protect you while you perform this service to her. I believe it will be your size."

I didn't like the word "service," but I stepped forward and took the shield anyway. I wasn't the jarl's sworn thegn. I would accept the gift as tribute, a gift between allies, not as payment.

Aslaug helped to adjust the red leather straps at the back. It fit perfectly on my arm, but I wasn't used to fighting with a shield. Before I'd lost my hand, I had delighted in using two axes. But that had been the showy method of a silly child and had cost me. Afterward, I'd been so determined to fight as before, to display my hook defiantly, that I hadn't even thought about purchasing a shield. I raised it experimentally and was surprised to find that it wasn't as heavy or cumbersome as it looked, despite the polished brass fittings.

"It suits you," said Jarl Honor. She brought her fingers to her lips and whistled. Her stable boy emerged from the trees leading a tall, golden mare. She wore a new saddle, made from the same red leather as the strap on my shield. Her flaxen mane blew wildly in the wind. I covered my smile with my hand as the boy walked her straight to me. I slung the shield across my back and took her reins. My men clustered around to get a better look.

"Pack your weapons and enough food to see you through tomorrow," I said. "We'll leave in an hour."

To my delight, no one asked questions. The crew nodded and trotted off in the direction of the guesthouse.

"For just one day?" the jarl asked.

I raised my arm. My tattoos were already rearranging themselves to show the terrain around the village beneath the distant mountain. "The tracking will be easy." I flashed her a confident smile.

* * *

THE JARL MUST HAVE SENT an emissary to the town, because every soul in Eyerfall seemed to be at the wooden gate to greet us. It seemed excessive to me as a reception for wolf-hunters, but I supposed the jarl wanted me to believe my "service" was valued. Children rushed up to us with flowers and fresh fruits. Women handed us stitched favors and pebbles carved with blessed runes; merchants gave us trinkets and charms from their stalls.

The attention made me uncomfortable. It was so overdone and clearly contrived by the jarl to make me grateful to her. My new mare shied when a blonde toddler darted between her legs. But my crew and the two ponies we'd brought along as pack animals seemed to be relishing the attention. Smyain held a fresh apple in his hand and went as red as the fruit when a buxom girl kissed his cheek. Torstein cupped a runestone reverently in his hands. One of the ponies nuzzled an elderly man, who fed him carrots from a market cart.

I had hoped to stop in the village, water the horses, and let the men have an hour's rest before we proceeded into the forest. But there was no way we would get any rest with all these people swarming us. We might as well finish the jarl's mission and get back to Djalsfor.

"Let us through, please." I gritted my teeth and forced a smile. "The sooner we pass, the sooner we can deal with your little wolf problem."

The villagers laughed. I didn't think that what I had said was particularly funny, but I guffawed along with them

Unhappy to be marched on so soon, the crew exchanged disgruntled glances. Torstein disentangled himself from a worshipper and gestured for the rest of them to do the same. Even after all our work together, they still looked to him for guidance sometimes. I hated it, but I was growing resigned to it. Torstein observed me closely and seemed to intuitively understand what I wanted from the men. Trygve lacked that skill. As much as I valued my boatswain and trusted him, he didn't know how to translate my shifting moods into commands the crew could follow. I didn't like Torstein and still believed he would kill me given half a chance, but he had uses.

I dug my heels into the golden mare's sides. She shot forward at a canter. Her responsiveness and speed were exhilarating. The men groaned behind us, but obediently broke into a run. I set my jaw and kept up the pace until we were clear of the village.

While I waited for the men to catch their breath, I consulted my markings. The wolf pack had a found a cave in the mountainside to use as their den. They would probably sleep during the day. If we could reach it before nightfall, we could easily ambush them before they woke to hunt.

At the edge of the forest, I dismounted. I couldn't fight wolves from horseback, so I gave the reins to Trygve. I hung my new shield from my new mare's saddle. I wouldn't need it against a few wild animals and I didn't want it to get dirty. I would anoint it with my enemies' blood first. Plus, I still hadn't learned to move without having it bang against my knees.

The trees hugged the mountain, creating a dense forest at its base, but nothing grew on the slick slate-gray slopes. Sneaking up to the wolves' cave would be more difficult with no foliage to hide us or mute the sounds of our footsteps. My tattoos showed that the cave was almost directly above us, but we couldn't climb the sheer mountain face.

I pressed my fingers to my lips to signal the men to be silent. The last thing I wanted was for the wolf pack to jump down on us. A wolf might not be able to kill an armed grown man, but it could inflict nasty wounds. The creatures were fast, with sharp claws and teeth. I needed all my men battle-ready when we set sail for my home.

As we crept through the trees, I crouched against the side of the mountain, hoping that my chain mail would blend with the stone. The crew followed suit, and even the horses seemed to tread with deliberate softness. The woods had an otherworldly silence, so different from my home on the coast, where the sounds of crying seabirds and crashing waves were as constant as breath. When Steinair stepped into a pile of orange and purple autumn lives, the crunch was as loud as a scream.

I led them in a circle around the base of the mountain until we found a gentler slope. The autumn sun was already starting to dip behind the peak. Tiptoeing to the horses, I tied their stirrups into knots to keep them from clanking as we moved. I beckoned the crew and began jogging up the slope.

The den stood beside a shallow pool. A stream trickled down the side of the mountain, feeding into the pool. A few trees grew out of the soil above the cave. It would have been a beautiful, idyllic view, but for the half-eaten sheep that lay by the entrance.

The animal's tongued lolled out of its mouth and maggots feasted on its exposed entrails. My mare's eyes rolled at the sight of the sheep, then she sniffed the air. Rearing and screaming, she fought to free herself from Trygve's grip on her reins.

Cursing, I drew my battle-axe. Now there was no way we could sneak inside and slay the wolves as they slept. Their own weapons braced, the crew formed a half-circle around me. We blocked off the cave. None of the wolves would be able to run around us. Smyain reached into his pack and drew out a flint and steel. He rubbed them together until sparks formed. He lit a torch and handed it to me. I threw it into the cave's mouth.

From deep inside the mountain, I heard claws scratch on stone. A wolf let out a howl, and the men beside me tensed. Smyain tossed another burning stick. We all waited, unsure how deep the cave was.

The scraping sounds drew nearer. A growl sounded. My axe trembled in my hand. The growl sounded too low and gravely for a wolf, more like a bear. I shook my head. The cave would amplify the noises inside it.

In a snarling streak of black and gray fur, four wolves erupted from the cave. Their backs stood as high as my chin. Their huge maws dangled open, showing two parallel rows of yellow fangs. Instead of front paws, they had hands like a man's, but covered in coarse black hair. The creatures didn't charge. They formed an arrowhead behind the largest of their group. He watched me with appraising, too-human eyes.

The welcome we'd received in the village suddenly made sense. No wonder they had laughed when I had mentioned their "little wolf problem." If any of the villagers had seen these creatures up close, they knew we wouldn't face normal wolves. I wondered if the jarl had known before she sent us, or if the leader of the village had downplayed their situation to encourage her to send aid.

The lead creature crouched and roared. The rocks beneath my feet shook.

"Fenrir," Torstein gasped.

The men backed away, opening our defensive circle. The fenrir were legends, creatures of Asgard, who had snuck through the cracks between worlds. They digested fear. My crew had followed me willingly when they thought we hunted simple animals. They might have stood with me in battle against other warriors. But the jarl wanted to know if they would stand firm against creatures of myth. They had already failed. Honor must have known about these wolves.

My golden mare screamed again and lashed out at Trygve with her front hooves. He dropped her reins, and she bolted down the mountain. My eyes followed her for a moment too long, watching as she disappeared with my beautiful new shield.

The lead fenrir leapt.

A scream tore from my lips before I could stop it. I raised my axe too late. My hook rose involuntarily to shield my face.

A whir of arrows flew over my head. The creature whimpered; the sound was more mortal than I had expected. Blood splattered my face as the arrows bit into the fenrir's flesh. My crew's aim was impeccable, but I didn't have time for pride. The fenrir tackled me, slamming into me with its full weight. I fell backward, hitting my head on a rock. The beast's sharp teeth closed on my calf. It shook its head from side to side, shredding muscle while I moaned. The pain made me wild. I slashed at the creature's belly with my hook, tearing its flesh open. I twisted in its hold until I could sit up. Then I brought my axe down on the fenrir's neck, severing its head.

Hackles raised, the other creatures formed a circle around me. Drool dripped from their jaws. They moved closer. I needed to get up, to get a better angle to swing with my axe, but my leg was a mess of torn muscle and exposed bone. Another arrow sank deep into the flank of one of the creatures. It snarled, jaws snapping inches from my face.

My crew would be able to save themselves. Thanks to Aslaug's help, their arrows flew straight and found their marks. But although they might help me from afar, none of them would risk their lives for me. Maybe even Trygve had grown sick of following me, sick of my temper and inability to let go of a hatred these men had never earned. The performance of comradery we'd acted over the past week hadn't been enough. Jarl Honor had seen it for the hollow thing that it was. I'd trusted that illusion, thought it would be enough to get me home. I was the one who had failed. If Ersel had been here, she would have rushed in. But I'd betrayed her, and now she wasn't here to save me.

I couldn't fight a whole pack of these creatures. I closed my eyes and hoped that the fenrirs would go for my throat, so I wouldn't have to feel them eat me. I remembered how I'd threatened to dangle Torstein over the bow of the ship with my hook through his eye socket and let the sharks devour him from the feet up. Was this a god's idea of sick irony? I wondered if Torstein would see it that way, once I was dead.

A battle cry sounded behind me. The fenrirs turned, and my crew charged. The creatures abandoned me and rushed toward the men. Pain made my vision fade at the edges. Men's shouts and animal whines blended. Blood made a sticky pool beneath me.

Soft, hay-scented breath caressed my cheek. I heard a whicker, and then a velvet nose nuzzled my hair. I looked up into the face of the dun pony I'd ridden to meet the jarl. I scooted backward until I found his front legs. He stood in place while I hauled myself upright. Pain shot through my leg but, by leaning on the pony, I managed to stay on my feet.

My crew were clustered around the carcasses of the remaining three fenrir. When they saw me rise, they trotted to me. They were covered in black blood. Steinair clutched at his arm, but their faces showed triumph. Why had they saved me? They had to know that my performance over the last week was for Jarl Honor's benefit. They could have let me die.

Trygve reached me first. "Gods, Ragna. Why didn't you move? It was as if you were frozen, and then that beast just jumped on top of you."

"I know. I got distracted by the horse."

"You all right?" Torstein pushed Trygve out of the way.

The sleeve of his red tunic was ripped. I blinked as spots blurred my vision, which shimmered like water. I was losing too much blood. "Why?"

Torstein raised an eyebrow. "Why what?"

"Why didn't you just run?"

"Where would we be without our grumpy captain?" His tone was teasing, and his eyes were gentle. But when he noticed my trembling chin, he sobered. "The styrimaðr who took you and sacked your home? We all know he was a bastard. Some of us have a pretty good idea of what you must have gone through. And Haakon? We didn't like him any better."

"Then why did you follow him?" I had asked almost all the other men to tell me their stories over the past few weeks, but I had never asked Torstein.

Torstein shrugged. "What choice was there? I was born in Bjornstad. My father was a scribe, but I was never any good at letters. The only other jobs were at the jarl's longhouse."

"But—" The sight of exposed bone and the smell of my own blood was making me nauseous. "You hate me."

"Maybe at first," Torstein agreed. He offered his arm. "But we are not all like the men who took you. Even Haakon thought Magnus—the styrimaðr who took you—was rotten. He picked him for the raid on your village. The rest of us? We never wanted any part in killing women and children. So Haakon chose Magnus for the job, knowing full well he was the only captain who'd do it. Magnus found a crew as dirty as him. All that man ever cared about was blood-sport and gold." He spat on the ground. "He had no honor."

Magnus. The name echoed in my ears. All this time, I'd never known my captor's name. The men who destroyed my town were nameless monsters, which made them even more terrifying and hateful in my memory.

Torstein shook his head slowly. "Light fire to a whole town while they slept? Round up and kill a group of children? Before I joined you, I fought in battles against seasoned warriors. I never killed a child or burned innocent people in their beds." He looked into my eyes. "I know you believe the worst of us, but we're not all the same."

Magnus. I thought of the styrimaðr stepping into the hold where Vidar and I had been kept in his long black cloak, the way he had cut off his own sailor's head without hesitation, and of Vidar's screams when they had thrown him overboard. Magnus had been a monster, but he was dead. My crew were not him.

I gripped the pony's back. I couldn't meet Torstein's gaze, so I looked over my shoulder at the rest of the crew. They were loading the fenrir carcasses onto the other pony. I was going to skin the one who had bitten me and wear his pelt as a cloak.

"Shall I help you up?" Torstein pointed at my leg. "You need to get that cleaned or it's going to fester."

I nodded, and he lifted me by the waist as if I were no heavier than a child, seating me sidesaddle so that my injured leg wouldn't have to grip the pony's sides. He tore off a section of his tunic—Haakon's tunic—and wrapped it carefully around my calf, binding my leg so the blood would stop. My leg stung where the skin had been ripped away, but Torstein's makeshift bandage helped.

I knew I should say something to acknowledge he was right, but the words were caught in my throat. The men who had kidnapped me would have run at the sight of the fenrir and left me to my fate. They'd had no loyalty even to each other. They might have intervened after I was too injured to ever resist them again. Haakon hadn't needed me to walk. He'd only wanted my magic. I kept my eyes down and ran my fingers through the pony's coarse mane. The golden mare was nowhere to be seen, but this brave little beast had dragged me away from a fenrir's jaws. He deserved the position of war mount.

"I'll call you Vaskr." I scratched his withers with my hook. The pony was fearless and deserved the name. His ears swiveled back, listening to me. "People won't think we're worth anything," I whispered to him. "A one-handed girl riding a farm pony. But we know what we're made of, don't we?"

I clucked my tongue, and Vaskr took a hesitant step forward. He turned to eye me, as if to make sure I wouldn't fall. The pony stopped beside Trygve, and my boatswain jumped up behind me. He wrapped both arms around me to keep me aboard, and we set off for the capital.

Mörsugur
The Bone Month
December

EVEN CARRYING TWO PEOPLE, VASKR could run faster than my crew could travel on foot. I was losing sensation in my lower leg. If it became infected, our journey to Brytten could be delayed by weeks. I held my arm out straight as I could, so Trgyve could follow the map and steer the pony.

Nausea made it hard to focus. Trees and farms whipped by in a green blur. Vaskr was breathing hard. His wind came in short puffs that looked like dragon smoke. I leaned into Trygve's warm, solid body and closed my eyes. I didn't want to vomit on my hero pony's neck.

Aslaug met us at the city gate. The húskarl waited with their arms folded, talking to one of the sentries. Trygve pulled the pony to a halt in front of them. When they noticed my injured leg, their face went white. Then they peered hesitantly around Vaskr's flank.

"Where is your crew?" they asked.

"If I say dead, will you be sorry?" I glared down at Aslaug. In the heat of the moment, when my survival had been in question, I hadn't thought about their part in the jarl's plan. But now that we were standing at the gate to her city with my leg a shredded mess of muscle and torn skin, anger bubbled up inside me. Aslaug had been training beside us for weeks. They knew my men and had helped them, taken food with them. How could they have let us walk into such an ambush?

"They're not." Aslaug rolled their eyes. But when I didn't respond, their voice dropped to a whisper. "They're not... are they?"

"No," Trygve said, taking pity on them when I stayed silent. "Ragna was injured, so we galloped back as fast we could. The men will be here soon."

"No thanks to you or your jarl." I growled. "Please inform her that I will dine with her tonight, and that, sadly, I will require another shield."

"Where is the mare?"

"Gone. I've decided this pony will do."

"The cart pony?"

"Better the cart pony than that cowardly, useless mare. Where did you find her? Was she the reject of the market?"

Trygve nudged me. I knew I was being rude, but after our encounter with fenrir, I didn't care. I clicked my tongue at Vaskr. The pony walked through the gate, toward the stable where he knew he'd find fresh hay. "And," I called over my shoulder. "Send a healer to the guesthouse."

"What was that?" Trgyve demanded when we had ridden out of the húskarl's hearing. "Aslaug has given us far more help than we had any right to ask for. They have practiced with us every day, despite all the other work I'm sure the jarl has them doing."

"They could have warned me."

"They are Jarl Honor's second in command. Their loyalty is to her. If you told me a plan in secret, do you think I would tell her?"

"That's not the point," I growled, but a flush crept up my neck.

By the time we reached the top of the hill, Vaskr was dragging his hooves. We'd travelled over six miles, much of it at full speed. He had more than earned a few days' rest. I would make sure the stable boy brought him extra oats.

Trygve lifted me from the saddle. My leg swung limply over his arm, and I stifled a cry. He carried me into the guesthouse, nudged doors open with his broad shoulders, and laid me on the bed.

"You'll have to cut off my trousers," I said and gripped the headboard to steady myself. I was seeing spots again. "And bring the water. Clean the injury as best you can. I don't know how long it will be before the healer arrives, if she comes at all. She left rather angry."

Trygve ran his hand through his hair and muttered, "Wouldn't it be better if a woman did that?"

"Do you see any women here?" I snapped. "Go on. It's not as though this is the worst off you've seen me, and we both know I've never been interested in a man."

He sat beside me on the bed and pulled out a small bronze dagger. Carefully, he cut away the fabric of my trousers, leaving my leg bare. I winced. The wound went straight to the bone, as I'd first thought. The muscle was gnawed away, but, though a tiny splinter of bone had broken off, the rest of it remained whole. I took a deep breath. If the healer could remove the shard, I might be back on a horse in a few short weeks.

Trygve dragged the water bucket across the room. He dabbed around the injury, cleaning away dirt, leaves, and dried blood.

I remembered the last time he had done this. His mother had pulled me from the sea, thirsty and wretched. I'd been at sea for a week, tossed by the waves in the tiny skiff Ersel and I managed to repair. Once I'd recovered my strength, I'd disguised myself as a merchant, peddling the trinkets Ersel had left in my little boat, and gone to Jarl Haakon's fortress. It had been evening. The jarl had been at his supper. His guards had seen in me what they wanted to see: a petite girl with a fancy, ancient hunting horn to sell, no one of consequence, never a threat. They'd waved me in and stood outside the door while I stabbed their jarl in the chest over a dozen times.

But Haakon had been faster than I'd thought an old jarl with gout would be. When I had first come in, he had been asleep. But his sword had lain beside his feet and in his dying breath he'd severed my hand just above the wrist. I'd fled through the window at the rear of the longhouse and collapsed on Trygve's doorstep again. He'd wanted to simply clean and bind the stump. The hook had been my choice.

"You should have trained as a healer," I said. My knuckles were white. Blood loss was making me cold and numb. I could hardly feel the cloth on my skin. "You seem to be doing this often."

Trygve sighed. "Yes, and I'd be happy to never do it again. But somehow, I think if I stay with you, I'll be cleaning a lot of wounds."

"You must not think very much of my fighting abilities."

He laughed. "I think the world of your abilities, but you try to fight everyone, and no one can." His expression sobered. "What will you say to the jarl tonight?"

"I'm not sure." I scowled. "She knew those weren't ordinary wolves. If she had said they were fenrir, I would have gone anyway. But why lie to us? Still, if she's ready to sail next week, we need her."

Yarra was waiting across the Northern Sea. Once I freed her, we could go anywhere. We could find Ersel, and the three of us could travel the seas together. The rest of my family was gone. Nothing tied me to Kjorseyrr. I'd told Honor that I would govern and send tribute. But if she couldn't be trusted to tell me the truth, then why should I keep that promise?

The bedroom door burst open. Aslaug rushed into the room, leading the same ornery old healer who had refused to treat Ersel. Jarl Honor appeared in the doorway a moment later. She hovered on the threshold, forehead creased with worry. Her hands twitched at her sides as if she couldn't decide where to place them.

The healer sat beside me and took the cloth from Trygve. She clucked her tongue. "Well, at least you haven't brought me to see that damned Loki-spawned creature—"

I slapped her. The room went silent, and the healer clutched her cheek. Trygve covered his face with his sleeve, as if so embarrassed he couldn't look at me. Aslaug's hand went to their sword, but the jarl shook her head.

"Do not," I ground out, "ever call her 'a Loki-spawned creature' again."

"I cannot work under these conditions," the healer whimpered. She turned to the jarl and gestured toward me. "How can you expect me to work on a violent patient? I was harassed the last time I came here as well, just for stating the obvious that human medicines might kill a… being of the ocean!"

Jarl Honor crossed her arms over her chest and rolled her eyes. "You have worked on much less agreeable patients outside the alehouses. How much gold do you want?"

"I am afraid for my personal safety—"

"You are not," said Aslaug. The húskarl stood behind the jarl and folded their arms as well. "The mermaid was a guest of the jarl. You had no right to speak that way about her, then or now."

The healer's chin jutted out, but she rummaged through her roll of supplies. She drew out a sachet of dried herbs and barked at Trygve to boil water. Even though I was furious with the jarl, I was glad of her presence. I didn't think the old woman would dare poison me in front of her lord.

She brewed an herbal tea that smelled of ginger and pine. I drank it at her instruction. A numbing, intoxicating warmth spread from my throat all over my body. My limbs felt suddenly heavy, as if I'd drunk too much wine, but my mind remained sharp.

"You've lost a lot of blood. You'll need to stay in bed for a few days," the healer said.

I nodded, then looked away as the she threaded a long, silver needle. The jarl finally moved from the doorway to sit on a chair beside me.

"You knew they weren't wolves," I accused.

"I knew you could handle them, and you did. Aslaug tells me your men are on their way now. No deaths."

"That's not the point. You chose to withhold information from me."

"You will not always know what you are up against," the jarl argued. "I wanted to see how your men would react when faced with unknown beasts, when victory wasn't assured. Given your condition, I'd say they must have fought for you."

"But you knew." I winced as the healer's needle punctured my skin. "You, as my ally, knew what you were sending us against and you lied."

"Yes, I knew and I didn't tell you because it suited my test, just as you knew the shapeshifter did not travel alone back to her people and chose not to tell me."

I stiffened. Loki had visited at night, and we had traveled by magic from the field to the guesthouse. I didn't think the god would have let themself be seen.

"I do not know what happened," the jarl continued. "But the story you told Aslaug, about Ersel returning to her people? She was sick, Ragna, so sick she could hardly move. The healer told us she would die. People so ill they can't stand up don't just evaporate into the night, shapeshifter or not."

"She returned home." My words were a yelp, as the healer tugged on the thread.

"Maybe, but how? If you don't want me to keep secrets from you, you cannot keep secrets from me."

"A thegn saw you go to the practice field alone the night the mermaid vanished," Aslaug cut in. "He said it looked as if you were praying. And then he heard you arguing with someone."

I brandished my arm at them. The maps showed the mountain where the fenrir had attacked, now with a fresh inscription of runes. "I'm gods-blessed remember? It makes sense that I would be pious. Maybe I was addressing Heimdallr."

"Enough," interrupted Trygve. We all turned to my boatswain, who was shaking his head. "We can't go in circles anymore. Neither of you has been fully honest. That's probably prudent. But if we are going to sail together, we need to start working together."

Aslaug and Honor exchanged glances.

"Are you finished with all your little tests?" I asked the jarl. "Have we passed?"

"Yes," said Honor stiffly.

"Then I will be honest with you."

"Leave us," I said to the healer. After the way she'd treated Ersel and the revulsion she clearly had for anything touched by Loki, I didn't want her listening to what I must say.

The healer cut the thread and packed her tools away. My skin was stretched over the wound, bound with uneven white threads. I shifted, and the stitches pulled. It reminded me of Loki's lips, bound painfully for centuries. The god hadn't told Ersel that I'd betrayed her. I didn't know what Loki's help meant, but I felt a bond with them now, a debt, even if I'd sworn no oath—assuming they had kept their word and Ersel was safe in the ocean.

The jarl already suspected that I'd had divine help with Ersel, but I didn't know what Loki would do once we reached my home. They had already helped me once, receiving nothing in return. The Trickster might decide to let us slay Haakon's men, only to have their creature devour us. Maybe I was wrong about their need of me. The god had waited centuries after all, and might think nothing of waiting until another child was born.

But if Honor believed that Loki was already on our side, I was sure she would put aside any misgivings about sailing with us. I could almost feel the ocean wind rustling through my hair again. I needed her ships. The truth wouldn't get them. I would tell her what she wanted to hear.

"I summoned Loki," I said, once the healer had gone. "Ersel is the way she is… a shapeshifter… because of a deal she made with them. The healer didn't know what to do. I thought they would be the only being who could help."

"You summoned Loki?" Jarl Honor echoed. "Just like that, and they came?"

"We have an understanding," I said. Some of the color drained from her cheeks, so I hastened to say, "An understanding. Not a bargain. I don't believe that Loki will stop us from taking back my town."

"And where did they bring Ersel? What did they do to her?" Aslaug asked.

I don't know, whispered an insidious little voice in my head. "They brought her to the sea. Djalsfor is too far away from the coast for her. She's a mermaid. Her body needs the ocean."

"And you promised them nothing?" Jarl Honor raised a skeptical eyebrow. "It does not sound like the god's nature."

"You're familiar with Loki? You have personal experience with their nature?" My tone was mocking, but I needed her to stop asking questions. The longer our exchange went on, the more likely it was that she would trap me in a lie.

Loki's nature was changeable; capriciousness was the very fabric of their being. In every legend, that was a constant. The god could be cruel or kind, helpful or destructive. No one, perhaps not even Loki themself, knew why they blessed some and cursed others.

The jarl flushed and looked at her lap. "No, I suppose not."

"My family's story and Loki's are entwined," I said. "You know that they're after the fragments of the dagger that can free their true voice. My family is both the solution to their problem and the origin. They will care for Ersel until we set sail, and then she will join us. Our plan will proceed as before."

The jarl's brown eyes searched my face. "I accept this."

"So, we work together?"

Jarl Honor nodded her head. She extended her hand, and I grasped it.

"We will take six ships," Honor said. "You and I will sail with a personal guard on my knarr so that we can plan our approach. Nominate one of your men to captain a smaller ship in your stead. I assume it will be Trygve? It is my gift, to replace the ship you lost."

I smiled. Even though she had not told me about the fenrir, if she had planned in this much detail, she must have expected me to return.

The outer doors to the guesthouse opened. My crew trudged inside. They flung their armor and weapons across the floor before they noticed the jarl. Torstein led them into my room.

"Well," he asked, a crooked smirk on his face. "Will you live?"

I studied him. He had proven himself and was not the man I'd imagined him to be when we first set sail together. Trygve had been with me the longest, and he was my shield-brother, but he couldn't command a ship the way Torstein could.

"Yes. I will recover. The damage to my leg isn't as bad as I first thought," I said. "The jarl has given us a ship. You will captain it."

His eyebrows furrowed. "Me? But you just said you'd recover."

"Yes. I will be sailing with the jarl to plan the landing of our entire fleet. Someone will need to watch over this lot." I gestured at the other men clustered behind him in the doorway. "I hold you accountable for their conduct and for the safe arrival of our new ship onto Brytten shores. Do you accept this post, styrimaðr?"

Torstein took a hesitant step forward. He chewed his lip; his whole expression seemed wary, as if he half-expected me to lure him into a trap. After the way I'd acted toward him, I couldn't blame him for his suspicion.

"If that is what you desire," he said carefully. "I would be honored."

"Excellent," said Jarl Honor. "Aslaug will prepare for our departure." She smiled at her húskarl. "They've been running errands and guarding me for too long. I know Aslaug is ready for a fight worthy of them."

Redness crept from Aslaug's neck to stain their pale cheeks. "It is an honor to serve you. I haven't complained."

"Of course not." Honor hoisted herself up from my bed and turned to face my men. "Aslaug is a warrior without equal in my jarldom. They are perhaps wasted staying at my side, but I wouldn't have them anywhere else. You have all proved yourselves today, in ridding us of the fenrir and saving your lord. You will make worthy allies."

Honor walked to the doorway. My men parted for her, then knelt respectfully as she passed. I expected Aslaug to go with the jarl, but the húskarl remained in my room. They went to the window and stared out at the city below the hill.

"Leave and close the door," I said to Torstein. "I need to rest."

My men filed out. When the door shut again, Aslaug sat in the chair the jarl had vacated. They pointed to the stitches on my calf. "Falkra is rude, but she does good work. The jarl doesn't keep her for her conversation. You should heal quickly."

"I expect to." I raised my hook. "And I'm not a stranger to fighting through pain."

"I suppose not." A grin twitched at the corner of their mouth. Then they rested their elbows on their knees, so our eyes were level. "I want you to know that I consider you and your crew my friends. I did not agree with Jarl Honor's decision to lie to you about the fenrir, but she is my jarl and whatever her decisions are, I must obey them."

"We'll work together," I said stiffly. "But don't expect me to like her."

Aslaug sighed. "I was born in Djalsfor. I've lived here all my life. But my grandfather was a traitor who ran from battle when he was called by Jarl Ulfric. My whole family might as well have worn a brand on our foreheads, the way his treachery marked us here. No one would trade with my father. No one would take my brother and I as apprentices. Even after my grandfather died, we still owed fines to the jarl for his crime. We could never raise the money to leave."

They poured a glass of water from the pitcher on my nightstand and handed it to me. "When Jarl Honor took the throne, she gave us a chance. No tests, no conditions. I made the most of it. Where other jarls would have kept me away from their person, and refused to let me advance, Honor has helped me rise. I'm the grandchild of a traitor, but no one scorns me now. Honor has made me rich and respected. If I ever took a spouse, I know that my family would not bear the stain of my grandfather's shame."

"And your brother?" I asked. "Does he serve the jarl also?"

"My brother took bribes from Jarl Haakon and sold secrets to him. Honor knew of the dagger, and the unique ability of those marked as navigators to recover it, long before Haakon did. She is a well-educated woman, interested in the histories and ancient texts. My brother is the reason Haakon learned of you. He rots in the dungeon under the walls, never to see daylight again. I don't petition for him. He was a liar and a coward. Because of him and so many others like him who would take advantage of her kind nature, the jarl has learned to be cautious. She tests now before she trusts."

When I said nothing, Aslaug continued. "When I first heard of your arrival, through Inala, I felt duty-bound to help you because of my brother."

"What he did wasn't your fault."

"No," the húskarl mused. "But we are all bound by the debts of our family, are we not?"

Their eyes scanned me acutely and I looked away. After what Loki had told me about Sigrid, I did feel a sense of duty toward the god. They had helped my ancestor and had suffered for it. The Jarl had said a thegn overheard snippets of my conversation with Loki and had reported to Aslaug. How much had the húskarl relayed to Honor? How much had they kept to themself?

Aslaug rose and clapped my shoulder. I winced.

"The jarl shows great trust by granting you an alliance, navigator. I know there are things you keep private. Because of my brother's role in what happened to your family, I do not bring these suspicions to the jarl's attention. But betray her trust, and I'll kill you myself."

The conviction in their threat startled me. I wondered if there was more at stake for Aslaug than simply their duty to their jarl. I realized how often I had seen them together, how personal Aslaug's interest in the jarl's wellbeing seemed to be, how their eyes never strayed from her when she was present. They were Honor's húskarl, but surely they could have delegated much of the work. There was no need for a steward of a great city to also function as a bodyguard, to carry things for her, or to personally assist her guests. Their brother rotted in prison, but I suspected another kind of love had taken the place of familial affection.

"You love her."

"What?" Aslaug barked a high-pitched laugh. "Well, yes, of course I do. She is my jarl. My life is hers."

"No. I mean you really love her. You want *her* to be your spouse."

"She can't be my wife, she's a jarl. If she marries at all, it will be a noble or another jarl, who will rule here while she raises children. She'll need political advantage."

Aslaug looked down at their lap; their long lashes blinked rapidly. I might have destroyed my own chance at romance, but I never would have let protocol or politics stand in my way. I'd kissed a mermaid after all, upsetting the conventions of both our worlds. Aslaug would never use or betray Honor. They proved that every day. The jarl should feel lucky to have someone so devoted to her.

I swallowed hard. Ersel had proved her devotion time and time again, and now I might have lost her. She deserved someone who valued her. Whatever I might feel about Honor, she valued Aslaug.

Taking another sip of my water, I said, "She's a ruler. A queen in her own right. She can have whomever she wants. She struggled and took her position. I've only known Jarl Honor for a brief time, but I can see that she has no plan to become a meek wife supporting a warlord husband."

"No, I can't see that either." Aslaug laughed, and their blush deepened. "That's part of what I like about her. And she is the most beautiful woman I've ever seen. I've been her thegn for nearly a decade."

"Have you told her?"

"Of course not. I would never burden her with my feelings."

"I thought you said your brother was the coward."

Aslaug stiffened and gripped the arms of the chair. "I am not a coward. I respect her. I don't want to impose myself or make things difficult for her."

"If she doesn't feel the same way, you never have to mention it again. But doesn't not knowing hurt more?"

When I was ten, I had professed my undying love to a girl in our town. My hands full of flowers from the meadow, I'd knelt in front of Silea and declared myself her thegn. The memory made me cringe, even now. Silea had been gentle but firm with my heart. She had her eye on the butcher's son. When my pride had recovered, we'd managed to stay friends. I'd found Astra soon after. Aslaug would respect Honor's feelings, but that respect shouldn't stop them from voicing their own—not when there was a chance.

The húskarl rose from the chair. They swept me an elegant, well-practiced bow. "I will take your words into consideration. Rest, navigator. You'll need your strength."

Mörsugur
The Bone Month
December

EIGHT DAYS LATER, WE SET sail across the Northern Sea. The jarl kept her word. She outfitted ten ships with fully trained warriors and handed an eleventh ship over to me. I'd been given a new sail, designed just for me: a black war-axe on a canvas of blue inked maps. It made me proud to watch *my* sigil billow in the sharp ocean wind.

The Sea Witch was a small, but beautifully made vessel. She was a snekke: a warship with no cargo hold and a draft so shallow she could be pulled directly onto the beach. Her decks were made of the same jewel-red wood as Honor's longhouse. The stempost had been intricately carved to show a mermaid pressing a hunting horn to her lips. Her form was too slender and, despite the long, elegant tail winding down to the hull, she had no scales. She shouldn't have reminded me so acutely of Ersel, when she looked nothing like the real mermaid I knew. But when I saw the horn at her lips, I blinked back tears and hurriedly bid Torstein a safe passage.

On the ride from Djalsfor to the coast, I had stupidly hoped that Ersel, her cheeks rosy and her eyes bright with health, might be waiting for us at the harbor. Either she was bound to the Trickster or Loki had told her of my betrayal and she wanted nothing more to do with me. I wasn't sure which fate was worse. I hated the idea of her being forced to carry out Loki's wishes, but I couldn't stand the thought of her choosing to abandon me either.

I joined Honor at the helm of her flagship. The huge knarr had a special throne built on the deck for the jarl to sit and watch the oncoming waves. I sat on the bench at her feet, but faced the oarsmen. Their hand resting on their sword hilt, Aslaug stood guard behind her. They dipped their head to me, but nothing about their posture betrayed the words that had passed between us. If Aslaug had confided their feelings to the jarl, neither of them gave any indication.

Shipbuilders on shore cut away the ropes binding the titan to the dock. The ship surged forward, driven by a powerful gust of wind.

I was going home, at the head of an army, having forged my own agreements with lords and gods alike. I should have been elated. I would avenge my family. I was going to see Yarra again. Instead, a heaviness settled inside me as the ship left the continent far behind. When we landed on Kjorseyrr's coast, my family would not be waiting in our house. Uncle Bjorn wouldn't tell me how proud he was. Mama wouldn't get the chance to scold him for putting dreams of the sea in my head as a child. Lief wouldn't run into my arms.

Ersel would not be waiting on the beach.

I left the bench and limped down the steps to the cargo hold. The jarl could manage the men on her ship without my interference. We were allies with a political bond, not friendship. The pony was my only true friend on board. Vaskr was stabled below deck in a narrow hold with two other horses: the jarl's gray stallion and Aslaug's mare. The stallion was squealing and trying to attract the mare's attention. Vaskr stood between them, seeming oblivious as he munched hay from a trough.

His small brown ears pricked up when he heard me coming. Honor's stallion reached into his trough to steal a mouthful of his hay. The jarl had offered to let me choose a new warhorse, but I had wanted a creature I trusted. The golden mare had not run back to her stable in Djalsfor. For all I knew, she could have been eaten by real wolves. I didn't mourn her loss. My leg had been healing well, but it still wasn't at full strength. Even though it would take another week to make the sea voyage, I didn't want a difficult horse who would exhaust me before the battle even started.

I slipped into his stall beside him, then sank down into the straw at his feet. Vaskr dipped his head down and blew sweet breath into my face. When I'd first seen him in Halvag's barn, I had dismissed him. Why was I always learning the value of things so late? I ran my hand down his cannon. He lifted his foot obediently, holding it up for me. I traced the metal shoe with my finger.

I missed Ersel. Now that I was back at sea, her absence left an ache. Since the day she'd come aboard my ship, I'd treated her like a weapon, an object to scare my men into submission. Our time together was full of stolen moments spent hiding below deck from the crew. Even then, I'd used her as a respite, so wrapped up in my own thoughts of revenge that I'd never even asked her if she missed her home. Coming on land for the first time should have been wondrous for her. It was a culmination of a dream she'd treasured since childhood. Had I ruined it? Had I really betrayed her out of love for Yarra? Or had everything, since the very beginning, been all about my revenge?

The pony slowly lowered his hoof. He nuzzled my hair. I took hold of his halter and pulled his face to my chest. I hugged his soft muzzle, and his warmth brought tears. I sobbed until my throat was raw and my stomach cramped. Vaskr stood still and let me hold him.

*   *   *

I STAYED WITH VASKR UNTIL I heard barrels being rolled across the deck. To keep the ale and water we had with us fresh, the crew would only open a few barrels at a time. If I missed this chance to drink, I'd have to wait until the next opening. I patted the pony's neck and then went to find the jarl.

Honor's sailors had fashioned a makeshift table for their jarl by pushing benches together and covering them with a white cloth. The table had been spread for three, with bread, strips of beef, and apples. At sea, most foods could be eaten without a knife or plate.

Honor held a clay bowl filled with strawberries in her lap. She balanced a goblet filled with what looked like wine in her brown hand. Aslaug sat on the bench at her feet holding a serving plate of dried meats. The húskarl didn't eat. Aslaug's pale skin had taken on a greenish hue, and they had purple rings around their eyes. I wondered when they had last sailed. The waves did not seem to agree with them.

Honor passed the bowl of berries to me. "We try to eat well on our voyages. We'll eat the fruit in the first days before it spoils. The styrimaðr says berries help us conserve water."

I took a handful of the strawberries. They were filled with juice and stained my palm red. "I can see that. When I last sailed, we only had salt fish, pork, and bread. I wasn't sure how long we'd be at sea, and our ship wasn't large enough to carry excess. When we lost a few of the water barrels, it was a disaster."

Aslaug pointed up to the knarr's enormous sail. "Have you ever been on a ship so large?" They sighed and clutched their stomach. "I'm finding the motion on this larger vessel does not agree with me. It is less bouncy than a drekkar, but the constant slow sway…"

Their voice trailed off and they ran to the ship's rail, leaving Honor and me to devour the rest of the food.

"We will need to decide where to land," Honor said, wiping her mouth on her sleeve. "We have enough warriors, I think, to storm the town head-on and win. But I don't want to waste lives if we can help it."

I nodded and peeled back the sleeve of my tunic. The jarl bent down for a closer look. The ink had darkened, almost to black. The markings had never changed color before. Our route to land extended from my forearm up my bicep. The waves surrounding our ship were oddly still. It was as if my desire to go home was so strong that the markings had become unchangeable, as if the magic were unwilling to show any other place until I achieved my aim.

Honor tapped a natural harbor shielded by a rocky mountain with her finger. It was a perfect location for our landing. She opened her mouth to speak, but then raised her head and beckoned Aslaug. The húskarl stumbled over on shaky legs. Their cheeks still looked green, but their eyes had come alive at being summoned, at being needed. They knelt beside me. The jarl pointed to the map on my skin again, then guided Aslaug's hand to the stretch of beach just above the obvious harbor.

I fought the urge to roll my eyes as the jarl said, "We haven't decided where to land. What do you think about here?"

Aslaug bit back a smile. They traced lower, to the cove. Their fingers brushed Honor's again. "What about there? It would give us more shelter and, if we disembarked at the right time, the mountain would hide us from view."

I pulled my arm back against my chest, no longer willing to function as a living game board for their flirtations. Aslaug must have told Honor about their feelings after all. From the look of things, they were reciprocated. At least some of us would be happy—if we survived the battle ahead.

"I'll inform the styrimaðr," Aslaug said. They rose to their feet and motioned to me. "You should come too, so we can show him. Is there anything else you need, my lady? I can fetch it for you?"

Honor raised her wine goblet to us. "I'm satisfied to watch the waves."

"You told her," I said as soon as we were out of the jarl's earshot.

Aslaug's cheeks colored. "Yes."

"And?" I made a beckoning motion with my hand. "It seems to be going well?"

"We decided to discuss it further after the battle," said Aslaug, but their wide smile betrayed them. "We will have more warriors, but with Loki's creature in the battle, we don't know what the outcome will be. The jarl will be heavily guarded at all times. But if I don't survive, I don't want her to think she owes me anything."

Shaking my head, I followed them to the rowing benches. The knarr's styrimaðr stood before the rest of the crew, barking orders at them. He was tall and lanky, boyish still, despite his age. Eirik was an experienced seaman who had been captaining Djalsfor ships longer than I'd been alive. My markings intrigued him, but he didn't trust magic alone to guide his ship. Everything I said had to be carefully verified on the vellum maps stretched out on a wide table below deck. Even then, he preferred to chart his own course where possible.

I presented my arm to him. Eirik studied the harbor, measured the distance to the town with his fingers, then grunted his approval. "Seems as good a place as any. But will it be deep enough for the knarr? I don't want to run her aground."

"At this time of year, it should be," I said.

"I'll confirm the location and send rowers to the other captains."

The knarr had two small skiffs suspended on ropes along its hull. They allowed Eirik to communicate quickly with the other ships in the jarl's fleet. All the other captains took their orders directly from Eirik. As soon as they saw the skiff in the water, they dropped their anchors.

"What should I do?" After only a day at sea, I was already growing bored. When I had captained my own ship, every moment had been an adventure. My status as the jarl's ally granted me a reprieve from the oars, but I had no crew to command. There was nothing to worry about, and after months spent constantly on edge, the lull made me even more anxious.

Aslaug wrapped their arm around my shoulders. "You rest your leg, practice with your weapons, and help me keep the jarl entertained. Her temper sours if she sits in a chair too long."

I laughed, pleased by the gesture of comradery. Aslaug would always be loyal to Jarl Honor first, but I valued our friendship.

Eirik moved to signal the messengers, but I held up my hand. "Wait. I want to add a note to Torstein's missive."

"Commands for your crew?" Aslaug asked. "Do you think Torstein has undermined you already? Surely, he wouldn't be so stupid."

"No." I called over my shoulder as I trotted toward the messenger. "I just want to tell him to keep his eye out for blue scales."

Mörsugur
The Bone Month
December

Eirik needn't have worried about the depth of the harbor. The weather in Brytten was uncharacteristically warm for winter. As we'd neared the island, I'd shed my fur cloak in favor of a lighter woven tunic. The snow on the mountain that overlooked the cove had started to melt; the edges of its white peak were bare and gray. The sea level had risen; the rocky beach was entirely submerged, and the waves crashed into heather. The trees still had their amber, gold, and pink autumn leaves. From afar, it looked as if the hills were blanketed in jewels.

We dropped the anchor. At the knarr's helm, the jarl stood with her arms held out while Aslaug draped chain mail over her wool tunic. The crew hauled an iron chest full of helmets, swords, and axes into the center of the deck.

"We will disembark and climb the western summit of the mountain," Honor said. "Our force will storm the town head-on. We will lure the bulk of the enemy force to us. Ragna and her men will seek out the keep."

I swallowed. Jarl Honor and I had made the plan last night. She would lure the enemy from their keep and fight them in the open field beyond the town. Their keep was made from wood. The structure would keep out the wild animals that roamed the mountains, but they couldn't barricade themselves inside without risk of being burned alive. Most of their force would rush to meet Honor's warriors. They might leave a guard or two behind to keep whatever prisoners still lived from escaping, but we could handle them. But Loki's creature would be in the keep too. It was up to me to figure out how to kill it or entice it to our side. If I failed, everything would be lost, even if Honor won on the field.

I prayed that Loki would decide to intervene.

As the jarl's men selected their weapons, I readied one of the skiffs. I would board the snekke with Torstein, and we would land it together. The small boat was eerily like the one I'd used to escape the shipwreck. I thought of Ersel floating on her back in the water beside me, watching as I rowed. She had been so at ease that day, with a bemused smile on her lips, cheeks flushed, and rich cerulean hair fanning out around her face.

Aslaug freed the ropes binding the skiff to the deck. It splashed into the water below. I paddled the distance between the flagship and *The Sea Witch*. The waves were shallow and gray. A few dirty-looking seagulls bobbed beside me.

I longed to see the glimmer of Ersel's lilac fins, but my own sea witch was nowhere to be seen. She wasn't going to come back. And for now, I had to forget her. We had a battle to win.

When I reached my ship, Torstein pulled me over the rail. The men were equipped and ready. Each of them wore a new tunic, designed by Halvag. It bore the same black axe as my sail.

Torstein clapped his hands, and the rest of the crew lined up for my inspection. I smiled and paced in front of them. They all looked strong and well-fed after the voyage. After a week at sea, my leg gave only the slightest twinge when I walked. We were as ready as we could be.

At my nod, the men rowed us to the shore. Unlike Jarl Honor's heavy knarr, my little snekke had a shallow berth. We could anchor right off the beach and disembark without skiffs or rafts. The jarl's forces would take time to cross the mountain. By the time they arrived, we needed to be in position to infiltrate the keep.

The ship ploughed into the sand. I leapt over the rail, landing knee-deep in the water. My new shield was strapped to my back. I carried a freshly forged battle-axe, light enough to be used one-handed; its blade had been sharpened to a dangerous gleam.

We left Trygve behind to make sure the ship did not drift. One of the jarl's crews would stay in the cove, their duty to protect our ships at all costs, just in case some of Haakon's men ventured over the mountains. Trygve only had to mind the tides.

Vaskr already waited for me on the beach. Despite his long journey, the pony stood still and quiet beside the raft the handler had used to bring him to shore. His eyes were wide, taking in the new world around him as his handler stroked his neck. Although I wouldn't ride him into the town itself, Vaskr would carry me over the mountain to save my leg. Pain brought its own kind of exhaustion. I wanted to be alert when I embedded my new axe in my first enemy skull.

I bent my knee, and Torstein boosted me onto Vaskr's back. Over the mountain rolled a dark thunder cloud, purple with its rage. Fog clawed up the rocks. From the south, the mountain would be almost entirely concealed. They would never see us coming. I smiled and patted Vaskr's neck. At last, I was going home.

*   *   *

AT THE BASE OF THE mountain, my town lay in ruins. All the houses were gone, burned to ash. The fields, once so carefully tended, lush and green, were a tangle of charred stubble and bones. Haakon's men had constructed a wooden longhouse in the town center, where a forge had once stood. A wall surrounded it, made from stolen stones, daub, and rotting timber. Two sentries paced in front of a crooked iron gate. A funeral pyre smoldered at the center of the town. From a distance, it was impossible to see the body that lay upon it, but I imagined my cousin's small frame and had to choke back a sob. The air still smelled faintly of smoke and burning hair.

We waited in the remains of a farm cottage at the edge of the town, pressed against a low stone wall, for signs of Jarl Honor's arrival. Her warriors would make as much noise as they could—I'd seen the wooden drums lined up on the knarr's deck along with the jarl's hunting horn—to draw the enemy's attention. I crouched beside the window, my legs already cramped. A few of the men fidgeted, but one hissed command had them standing as still as statues. We must not be seen. Alone, we would be slaughtered.

The handler hid with Vaskr in a cave just beyond the village. The man had seemed frightened and restless, as though he might flee to the safety of the ships at any moment. So I had told him that, if I returned to find him alive while my pony was not, I would drag him to Norveggr behind the ship like a prized catch. Torstein had chuckled at the now familiar threat, but the handler had gone whiter than milk.

The hunting horn blew in the distance. The sound it emitted was high and sinister, like a valkyrie's scream. The sentries opened the gate and fled into the fortress. They left the gate ajar. The hairs on my arms stood up. The pit of my stomach dropped.

The mountain roared with Honor's battlesong. Torchlight flooded through the open gate. Haakon's warriors erupted from the keep, banging swords and axes against their shields as they raced toward the sound. Loki's creature did not run with them.

I held my breath until the last of the warriors streamed from the keep. Smyain stepped forward. He hoisted the shield from my back, then secured it to my arm. He placed my horned, iron helmet on my head and buckled the strap beneath my chin. My heart pounded so fiercely that I felt lightheaded, but the shield's weight comforted me. Still crouching, I beckoned to the men.

We crept out of the farmhouse, hiding in the shadows of blackened buildings until we reached the gate. I put my fingers to my lips. There would still be guards inside. If we were to fight Loki's creature, none of my crew could fall to human swords.

The gate led to a narrow, winding hall with damp walls that seemed to close in around us. The inside of the fortress smelled of rot and mold. My breath echoed inside my helmet. My crew were as silent as cats, moving a single step at a time, weapons held ready. From somewhere deep inside the keep, the sound of laughter reached us.

"We're the lucky ones," a deep voice said. "All we have to do is sit here and watch the brats. Did you hear those horns? It's a proper army this time, not those little raiding forces sent by Jarl Thorn."

"We don't even have to watch them. Not with the beast here," returned his companion. "Shall I fetch another round of ale?"

The fortress followed a design that I knew. Several of the jarls in Brytten had holds like this. The entry way wound around the central hold in a spiral before feeding into the keep. The narrow halls kept enemies from rushing in an organized line. Light from the central keep spilled out into the hall, creating shadows. Once we rounded the next corner, we would be in the heart of the longhouse, visible to any straggling enemies.

I pressed my back against the wall, my axe held to my chest. Our footfalls suddenly seemed as loud as shouts to me. Signaling to my men to stay hidden, I peered around the corner.

Two warriors sat playing dice at a table. As I studied them, my blood ran cold. I recognized one of the men. He wore an eye patch over his left eye and had two matching scars running down his cheeks like tears from my nails. He still wore a faded, dirty red tunic, emblazoned with Haakon's sigil. It was the same man who'd grabbed me the night the raiders came. He and his companion had killed my family in their beds.

I wanted to rush forward to slice open his belly with my axe and spill his guts over the wooden floor. But a long shadow cast on the floor behind them kept me motionless. I peeked around the wall again, looking for the source of the shadow. A large horse stood behind the game table; its head was partially submerged in a feeding trough. It was pure white with a light pink muzzle and electric blue eyes. It had eight legs instead of four, with cat-like paws in place of hooves. When it lifted its head, a man's arm dangled from its muzzle. Golden rings still decorated the man's hand. The creature chewed it absently, its great jaws grinding the bone as easily as hay.

The Sleipnir. I recognized it from the stories Mama had told me as a child. Once the valued steed of Odin, the beast had been born of Loki's own flesh. They had given natural birth to the creature and it was the strongest of their beasts. It had lived for centuries and had survived against powerful enemies. It stood over a trap door. I knew with sickening certainty that was where we would find the children. If I wanted to get to Yarra, I had to defeat a creature that feasted on human bones.

We would have to charge together. Separate, we had no chance of survival. Even together, my small band of men might not be enough. I considered falling on my knees and begging Loki for intervention.

Smyain tiptoed closer to me, then pulled his bow over his shoulder. He nocked an arrow and aimed it at the nearest warrior's heart. Carefully, I repositioned his elbow so that the arrow would strike the other guard. Whatever the eight-legged horse might do, the man who had killed my brother was going to die at my hand. An arrow to the chest was a mercy he did not deserve.

The arrow flew and struck deep. The one-eyed guard shouted as his companion slumped and fell from his chair. The arm dropped from the Sleipnir's mouth, and it pivoted toward us. Steinair stepped out into the keep and raised his sword. His legs were shaking.

"Reckless boy," Torstein cursed. He lunged for the back of Steinair's tunic, but it was too late.

The Sleipnir's eyes narrowed; it crouched like a great cat. Then in a flash of cyan smoke, it struck. The creature's jaws closed around Steinair's skinny neck, snapping his head from his body. It rolled toward us, eyes still wide. The Sleipnir hauled his body— its new prize—to the feeding trough and deposited the corpse inside. I covered my mouth. Steinair had been little more than a child himself, not even sixteen. I should have left him on the ship with Trygve, whatever his skill with a sword.

"Come out and play, cowards," the guard called. He banged his sword against the table. His voice was so hauntingly familiar. It had been half a year, but I remembered his hot breath against my cheek and the way he had held me against his chest, blade at my throat.

The men at my back glanced at the hall behind us. The Sleipnir moved like nothing I'd ever seen. No wonder Haakon's men had dared to leave only two warriors behind. The remaining guard rose from the table, holding his sword outstretched. He snapped his fingers, and the Sleipnir grudgingly turned its head. Its eyes fixed on us. I sensed that it could see where we crouched, even through the walls. If we tried to run, none of us would make it out alive. We needed more men—another army maybe—to defeat it.

Or one god.

My crew had proved themselves. They had risked their lives defending me from the fenrir. If I wanted to be worthy of their loyalty, I had to be willing to sacrifice too.

"I'll do it," I hissed, not knowing if Loki could even hear me. "I'll make a deal with you."

The silence that followed made my stomach curdle. The Trickster was content to wait for another navigator after all. We weren't going to get out. We were all going to die here. My men had finally started to respect me, and I'd led them straight into a trap.

"All the pieces?" The voice was soft, rustling past my ear like leaves on an autumn wind.

"All of them. Just call your beast away." I nearly trembled with relief.

"If you try to break our bargain, I will send the Sleipnir to hunt down and devour anyone you have ever spoken to. Your crew. Your cousin. The old man who weaves. Even into the ocean to devour your pretty mermaid." A glimmer of light appeared at the corner of my vision, hovering like a specter.

"I won't back out."

"I believe you," said Loki. "But it never hurts to have guarantees."

The god's form solidified. They appeared as a burly, muscled warrior with a long, braided, blond beard. They clutched a cyan shield in their hands and wore antlers so tall they nearly scraped the low ceiling of the fortress. My men jumped back, their eyes wild. A few fell to their knees.

The Trickster brushed past them. They walked confidentially into the center of the keep. A genuine, affectionate smile lit their face at the sight of the creature. The Sleipnir cocked its head. Haakon's guard sneered. "One warrior?" he called down the hall. "You send one warrior to face our beast?"

Loki laughed. The voice that emerged from their lips now belonged to a child, not the formidable warrior standing in the keep. "Our beast," they giggled.

The color slowly drained from the warrior's face. He stepped back, using the table to shield himself. Loki tapped their cyan shield and held out their hand. The surface of the shield rippled like the water of a pond. Nostrils flared, the Sleipnir prowled over to them. Then it dropped its blood-stained muzzle into the Trickster's outstretched palm. Loki reached up to pat its neck, and the creature vanished.

Loki turned to me and smiled. Their shield bore a new decoration. A great white horse with eight monstrous legs galloped across the face.

The warrior fell to his knees. "You… we had a deal. The hersir made a bargain."

"Yes," said Loki. They jerked their head toward the corridor, toward me. "And she offered me another one. I have never once gone back on a promise. Your hersir bargained for a creature to guard these children against invaders. I supplied such a creature, but we did not agree how long you could keep him."

Beckoning to my men, I stepped out into the light.

"I will be back," the Trickster said to me. "To claim what you owe."

Loki evaporated, along with his new shield, into a cloud of a cyan smoke. A vicious smile stretched my lips. I bared my teeth. I might have sold my life to Loki, engaged myself to a service that might take years, but the only thing on my mind now was the enemy who had killed my brother. I was going to savor my revenge.

Sword falling from his hands, the warrior stumbled back against the fortress' wall. "Mercy," he whimpered. "Take me prisoner. I'll serve your jarl."

"You will serve no one." I yanked my helmet from my head. My white-blonde hair fell to my shoulders. He looked into my face, then let out a cry of recognition.

He fell to his knees at my feet. I kicked him into the wall. He threw his arms up to cover his face.

"Hold him," I yelled to Torstein. My warrior looked sidelong at me, his eyes questioning. The enemy was unarmed now, and I could have ended it in a second. A single blow to the skull with my axe would have been enough. But I didn't want to. This was the man who had come into my home, who had killed my brother in cold blood. I was going to take my time. Maybe this would finally be enough to quench my burning thirst for revenge. Maybe after I did this, I would finally find peace.

Torstein seized the man's arms and yanked them to the side. I stepped over him, planting a foot on either side of his writhing body. Then I angled my axe and slit open his belly.

"Ragna…" Torstein whispered, his teeth gritted. He'd never used my given name. Even when he had hated me, it had always been "girl" or "you." For the barest second, it was enough to make me pause. "This isn't honorable."

I had once believed Torstein to be a murderer, capable of slaying women and children in cold blood. I had been so wrong about him. He still maintained a code, a sense of honor, that I'd already lost.

"This man." I pointed my axe at the warrior's chest while he screamed, and blood poured from the wound in his abdomen.

"Came into my house in the dead of night and murdered my seven-year-old brother in his bed. He and his companions killed my parents. He does not get off easily."

Torstein took a deep breath. He turned his head to the side. "Get on with it then."

"No!" the man shrieked.

My first cut had been shallow, only deep enough to break through the skin. The warrior moaned as I crouched down and whispered, "My brother was seven. Seven. He was gentle. Think about that."

I slipped my hook into the opening in his stomach. Muscle and blood squelched around my arm. The man writhed, as his legs desperately scraped the floor for purchase. I pulled my hook out; his bowel dangled from it like an oversized worm. Ignoring the smell and the blood that seeped through my fingers, I unwound it like a rope, then slung it around the man's neck. I pulled it tight, cutting off his cries. His face went purple. I kept up the pressure until he stopped twitching.

Torstein just stared at me; his whole body was rigid.

Smyain stepped forward, pushing his way through the line of men. He sighed and kicked the warrior's corpse aside. My lungs felt like ice. I started to shiver. A strange emptiness filled me as I looked at the smear of blood on the floor, then at the dead man's purple face.

There was justice in what I'd done, so why did I feel like this? It had to be battle fever. It was the only explanation.

He was gentle. My own words echoed in my mind. Whatever the man's crimes against him, Lief never would have condoned what I had just done.

Smyain ripped off a piece of his tunic. He wiped the blood off my face, both of my arms and hook. "There," he said, his voice a little strained. "Good as new."

"He will haunt you," Torstein murmured. "You're not a monster. The manner of his death will haunt you."

"He already haunted me." I knelt beside the trapdoor. "Maybe now, he'll finally be quiet."

Mörsugur
The Bone Month
December

SMYAIN BROUGHT ONE OF THE torches hanging on the keep walls. He shone the light down as I felt along the surface of the trapdoor for a handle or a lock. My fingers slid into a narrow keyhole.

"Search them," I said, pointing to the two corpses with my axe. "One of them will have a key."

The crew turned the bodies over and began rummaging through their clothing. I knelt beside the door again and pressed my lips to the keyhole. "Yarra? Are you in there? Can you hear me?"

I could hear something moving in the space below. But no voices answered me. What would I say to Yarra when I saw her again? She probably thought I was dead, or that I'd abandoned her long ago.

Smyain rushed to my side. He triumphantly brandished a little bronze key, sticky with congealed blood. "It was on the first one," he said.

I took the key and fit it into the lock. I didn't know what to expect. If the children had been confined and alone under the keep for more than six months, they would be scared and malnourished. What we would do if they were too sick to travel? While Honor met the soldiers in the meadows, we were supposed to get the children to the safety of the mountains before the battle moved into the town.

I yanked open the hatch. The smell of excrement hit me immediately. I covered my mouth and nose with my tunic. How could anyone keep children in a place like this? A set of wooden stairs led down from the trapdoor. There was no light coming from the space. I grabbed the torch from Smyain and descended the stairs.

A group of small, dirty figures huddled in the corner farthest from the steps. I walked toward them, holding the torch to light the way. My men started to climb down behind me. One of the children whimpered.

"Stop," I said. "Stay up there. None of them will know you."

At the sound of my voice, one of the figures broke away from the group. He was a boy of six or seven. I recognized his freckles and ginger hair, though I couldn't recall his name. He had been one of Lief's more regular playmates. I'd seen him countless times with my brother, skipping stones, singing, carrying buckets for Uncle Bjorn's forge. The clothes he wore were torn and filthy. His face had lost its roundness. His eyes looked impossibly large in his gaunt face. I crouched, and he approached me.

"Ragna?" he asked. One of his tiny hands reached out to touch my cheek. I felt suddenly ashamed that I didn't know his name or who his parents had been. I hadn't paid enough attention to

Lief when he was alive, or I would have known more about his friends.

The rest of the group unfurled like petals. There were only a handful of them—all younger than ten, all dirt and skin and bones. I had expected more children. How many houses had the raiders burned before they reached my family that night?

Where was Yarra? I scanned the torchlight over them, praying. But in my heart, I already knew that if Yarra had been there, she would have thrown herself at me.

I licked my dry lips. "Where is my cousin?"

Lief's playmate shook his head. "She's never been down here."

"Are there any others still alive?" I hesitated and my voice nearly broke. "Did you see… bodies?"

The boy studied his feet. "They made us watch when they burned the bodies. Yarra wasn't there either. And when they rounded up all the horses, Mjolnir was gone too."

Mjolnir would not have gone anywhere without Yarra. He was entirely dedicated to one little girl. Yarra would have died before she left that horse behind. I had spent the last few months justifying every action with concern for my cousin. Was it possible that she had never needed me to rescue her at all? Yarra had always been the toughest of us. But she was still only a child. Even if she had managed to escape amidst the chaos that night, how long could she survive on her own, in winter?

"Ragna?" Torstein called from above. His face appeared through the hatch. "We need to get them out of here. If the unlikely happens, and Honor loses, we need to be far away."

"We're coming," I shouted.

Once we hid these children in the mountains, I would go in search of my cousin. Whatever had happened to her, she was beyond the reach of Haakon's men.

*   *   *

THE FORT WAS SURROUNDED. WHEN I opened the front gate, chaos had broken out in the town. Jarl Honor's warriors pushed the enemy through the streets toward the harbor. The sounds of clashing iron and men's cries were everywhere. Bodies littered the streets; blood and mud churned together forming pools. Most of Haakon's men had stopped fighting and were running toward the three drekkar ships stationed at the town docks. I couldn't make out Aslaug or Honor in the fray.

Torstein grabbed the nearest child and hoisted her onto his back. The others followed his lead, each lifting a child. Our way to the farmhouse was blocked by two warriors circling one another with swords in hand. One of them still wore Haakon's colors. I sized up the distance between us, then threw my axe. It embedded in the back of the enemy's skull. He dropped to his knees, dazed, and Honor's thegn lopped his head from his shoulders.

"Get away from the water!" someone screamed.

I turned to the beach. The enemy warriors were wading into the ocean, scrambling for their ships. But as they ran through the waves, something pulled them under. A turquoise-scaled hand reached out from the water to grab an enemy's ankle. He fell into onto the rocks and was dragged into the ocean. A cloud of blood bloomed in the sea, followed by a flash of lilac. Something like hope made my chest flutter.

"Take them to safety," I said to Torstein. "I will meet you at the boats when this is over."

"That wasn't the plan," he argued. "We're supposed to get back. You're supposed to come with us. The jarl has this won. I'm not leaving you here."

"We did our part. The Sleipnir is gone." I pointed to the ocean and smiled, as another enemy vanished beneath the red waves. "She came back."

He shielded his eyes with his hand and squinted toward the water. A red-finned merman with black skin breached the water and tackled an enemy. Torstein sighed. "Trygve is going to panic if we come back without you."

"I'll be fine." I clapped him on the back. "And if I'm not, you get what you always wanted."

"I haven't wanted that in a while," Torstein grumbled. He hoisted the girl he was carrying higher onto his back. "We'll see you soon."

I nodded, then turned to the beach. The remaining enemy soldiers were clustered at the docks, caught between Honor's arrows and the merfolk waiting to drown them. Only a handful remained. I watched the water for Ersel.

Jarl Honor pushed past her front line of soldiers. Her armor was covered in blood-splatter and mud. She wrenched off her helmet and thrust it into Aslaug's waiting hands. Her black hair had been braided into an efficient knot at the back of her head. She had a small cut beneath her eye, but otherwise looked unharmed.

I closed my eyes with relief. They were both alive and would return to Djalsfor to forge whatever future they chose together.

The húskarl walked a step behind the jarl. They angled their shield so that it covered Honor's torso rather than their own. Together they approached the enemy.

"Kneel," Honor commanded the remaining fighters.

In the ocean, the merclan treaded water and listened. Ersel floated beside Havamal and a green-scaled mermaid wearing a diadem of sea pearls and white shells. The water around the merclan was murky with blood. Corpses floated on the shallow waves.

When Ersel saw me, she smiled and waved her webbed fingers. Hesitantly, I smiled too. She'd come back for me, yet a niggling voice in my head insisted things wouldn't be the same as before she had left. My hand drifted to the pouch at my belt; her stolen sea pearls were tucked inside. I needed to apologize to her.

"Will you give us your word to spare us? We demand your promise," shouted one of the enemies. He was slim and drenched with sweat. He held a bow and pointed an arrow at Honor. Aslaug stepped between them.

"I don't like your tone," the jarl snapped. "I will not spare you, but if the others yield now, their lives will be spared."

The other enemy warriors were on their knees in an instant. The archer looked around wildly, then ran at the jarl. Aslaug stepped in front of her. In a single, fast stroke, they severed the archer's head. I'd never considered decapitation a romantic gesture, but Honor's cheeks flushed. She smiled shyly at her húskarl.

A cheer went up from Honor's tired soldiers.

I approached them, wiping sweat from my face.

When she saw me, Honor's jaw tightened. "Is it done?" she asked. "Where are your men? Is the creature still alive?"

A murmur of panic whispered through the thegns around us. "It's gone."

Her eyes narrowed. "Gone but not dead?"

"It won't be coming back to bother us," I said. "Not unless I renege on my side of the bargain."

"And what are the terms of that bargain?"

"You know what they're after." I glanced at the warriors around us and dropped my voice. "I have to find it. Loki wants their true voice freed."

The jarl sighed. "I thought it might come to that. Once, I thought I might ask you to find it for me, but I realized on our journey that you'd never agree to that." She gestured to the charred buildings behind the beach. "As long as it exists, none of you are ever going to be safe. You may take the ship I gave you. I will nominate another steward to govern here until your return."

The jarl's thegns marched chained prisoners past us. They shuffled in the heavy manacles and kept their gazes trained on the bloody ground.

"What will you do with the prisoners?" I asked.

"We will use them to negotiate. Even now that Haakon is dead, thegns from his provinces still raid my borderlands. These men are the sons and brothers of some of those thegns."

"So they won't be punished at all." Petulance seeped into my voice.

"Building peace is sometimes more important than retribution—something you're going to have to learn as governor here." Honor said. "I'm going to send settlers to help you."

"What?"

"You saw Skjordal. There are entire towns in my province with nothing left, soil that doesn't yield. I'm going to send those people here. They're hardworking and they won't cause trouble. You can't rebuild this town with only children and a few sailors."

I would be governor of a real town, responsible not only for a group of children, but for farmers, craftsmen... people's whole lives. When I'd made my proposal to Honor, part of me hadn't grasped what being a governor would entail. The town was in ruins. All those people would need homes and food we didn't have. I could lead us to fresh water, to deer and wild boar. But a few deer weren't going to feed an entire town through the coming winter. Even with settlers, I wasn't sure we had a chance. My shoulders sagged.

"It will be fine," said the jarl, noticing my expression. "These people know their trades. They will be a help to you."

"Halvag." An old weaver might not be very useful, but he had claimed me as his kin. I had a duty to him now. "I want my kinsman with me."

"And your cousin?" Honor asked hesitantly. "You haven't mentioned her. Is she... well?"

"She's missing, but alive. The other children say that she was never taken at all." Yarra would be alive. She had to be.

Torstein must have alerted Vaskr's handler to the battle's outcome, because he stood a few paces away. Hands shaking, he led the pony around the bodies that littered the streets. Vaskr paid no more heed to the corpses than he would to stones in his path. He stepped nimbly around them and nickered at me. The handler thrust Vaskr's reins into my hand, turned aside, and vomited. One of the thegns led the jarl's stallion forward.

"Honestly, Walden." Aslaug shook their head at the handler. They held fast to the stallion's bridle while Honor vaulted astride. "Why did you volunteer to come? Someone else could have looked after the jarl's horses here."

The handler flushed. He wiped his mouth, then lifted his chin to glare at Aslaug. "The jarl's horses are my duty."

"He manages them like no one else." Honor gave the handler a fond smile. She pulled a red cloak from the stallion's saddlebag and slung it over her shoulders. It fell elegantly over her horse's rump.

I mounted, and we trotted together to the town outskirts. Aslaug jogged beside the jarl's horse, still holding their bronze shield. Even now, when the battle was won and the enemies our prisoners, the húskarl wouldn't take chances with Honor's safety.

We stopped at the edge of the moor that framed Kjorseyrr's eastern edge. To my surprise, a flock of shaggy, long-tailed sheep still grazed there, oblivious to the fate of their owners. They bleated as we approached and circled around the horses. A bolder ewe nudged my foot, looking for grain.

"Your future citizens," Honor said solemnly.

We all burst out laughing. The jarl leaned over in her saddle and hugged me. The unexpected gesture made a sob rise in my throat. I coughed to banish it. "You're home," she whispered, solid arms holding me tight.

"If you see Ersel, tell her I'll be back soon," I sniffled. "And thank you."

WHEN ASLAUG AND THE JARL had disappeared over the hill, I took a steadying breath and pushed back my sleeve. The tattoos had returned to their normal, deep-blue color. The map depicted was familiar: the angular mountain peaks, the jagged coastline, all as they had been a thousand times when I'd ridden Fjara into the hills, looking for an adventure.

Yarra, I thought. Nothing shifted. Cold fear twisted in my stomach like a knife. What if the other children had been wrong? I imagined Yarra's small, charred feet protruding from a pile of smoldering bodies. That couldn't be. The children remembered Mjolnir, and he was gone. They had fled together. They must have.

Yarra. I pleaded with the magic this time. Yarra was not a navigator. If she had escaped, had she found shelter? Water? Food? I'd been so proud of her for escaping, I'd never considered how she might have survived afterward. Tough as she was, she was still a child. The idea that my cousin might have escaped, only to face a slow death from thirst and starvation was too much.

The skin above my wrist started to prickle. The tattoos shifted; the change was as slow as ice creeping over the surface of a pond. When I was tired, sometimes the magic didn't come swiftly. I held my breath as the markings revealed a forest grove a few miles away. I knew it well. A shallow stream ran through a clearing in the grove. When we were younger, Mama had taken all of us there to learn to swim. There was a natural cave in the hill beside it. Snowberries and wild carrots grew in the woods around it.

I nudged Vaskr, and the pony sprang into a gallop. A few sheep tried to follow us, but after a week aboard the knarr, Vaskr was ready to run. His bounding strides ate up the ground beneath us. When I'd ridden Fjara through these fields, I'd always had to stay focused on her. My mare had been strong and fast, but she spooked at shadows. I had to think ahead of her nerves, anticipate her. This brave pony would run anywhere I asked and never balk. I wondered how I'd ever thought he was worthless.

When we neared the grove, I dismounted. If Yarra heard galloping hoofbeats, she might panic. She might run or hide so well I'd look right past her. The storm clouds finally opened, and the rain came down in fierce rivulets. Firelight emanated from the cave mouth and bathed the earth in a flicking, soft glow. Swallowing hard, I led Vaskr toward it.

A golden stallion flew at us from the cave's mouth. He lunged at me with his teeth bared and his ears pinned flat against his head. He reared, striking with his front feet.

"Mjolnir!" I shouted, throwing up my hand. "It's me. Stop!"

At the sound of my voice, the horse stilled. His nostrils flared. My gaze swept over him. Where his coat had once been as shiny and smooth as new bronze, now it was matted and marred by cuts. His stance was uneven; three deep puncture wounds were visible on his haunches, as if he had been struck with a mace. A flap of skin dangled from his shoulder.

I hummed softly to him and reached for the rope dangling from his head collar. I pressed my knuckles against his skin. His shoulder was burning to the touch, infected. It was a wonder the stallion hadn't died already from the fever. They had not escaped quietly and they had been hunted. The stallion's injuries all showed different stages of healing. If Yarra was alive now, it was because Mjolnir had fought their way to freedom.

"Ragna?"

The sound of her small, unsure voice made my eyes sting. I turned. Yarra stood at the edge of the clearing. She carried an armful of damp firewood and still wore her woolen nightdress, soaked from the rain and covered in mud. She dropped the wood at her feet. I fell to my knees and opened my arms.

She ran to me. I pressed my lips to her wet, blond hair. She felt painfully thin in my arms. A shudder passed through me, and tears welled in my eyes. If I had come a month later, after the frost had settled, she would have been gone.

We clung to each other and sobbed. I still had a bargain to keep, but for her the ordeal was over.

"How did you escape?" I murmured, still refusing to let her go.

Yarra stiffened in my embrace. "My father. He heard what was happening outside and he made me hide in the forge. I waited until I couldn't hear anything in the courtyard and then I snuck into the barn to get Mjolnir." Her voice trembled, and my heart broke. "They killed Papa, but they never found me. We tried to get into town a few times to get supplies. That's how Mjolnir got hurt."

Her small fingers reached for my hook and grasped it. "What happened to you?"

"I lost my hand in a fight."

Yarra's cheeks dimpled. "So, you did it? You're a warrior now?"

I tapped my chest proudly. "A styrimaðr. I have my own ship."

"I knew you would." She shook her head. "Even if you can't ride."

I rose from my knees and scooped her up and over my shoulder. Yarra squealed with laughter as I carried her to Vaskr. "Never repeat that to my men!" I said. "I have a reputation to protect."

Yarra slid onto Vaskr's back and wrapped her arms around his chubby neck. "He's cute."

"He's the best warsteed I've ridden," I said.

"If your mama heard that," Yarra giggled.

Her voice trailed off. Her eyes met mine, and we both fell silent. I grabbed Mjolnir's lead, then jumped onto Vaskr's back behind her.

"They've gone to Valhalla. It's just us now, and we've got to do what we must." I nudged Vaskr with my heels.

* * *

BY THE TIME WE RETURNED to the town, Jarl Honor was already setting things in order. Her thegns had gathered the enemy bodies and burned them on a pyre. Tents for the soldiers had been pitched in the stubble fields. The fortress' keep had been cleaned and scrubbed. Walden took Mjolnir and Vaskr to the remains of my family's barn. The stallion had flattened his ears, but, after a scolding from Yarra, had followed Walden to have his wounds cleaned.

A tent had been set up for me. Smyain met me at its entrance with a tray in his hands. He swept me a bow that made Yarra giggle before setting the tray on the floor for her. It was laden with sheep's milk, bread, and cheese. She tore into the bread like a starved dog, pausing only to gulp milk. When she had finished, I tucked her into a bed of wolf pelts. Smyain knelt beside her.

"I'll watch her. You should let the jarl know you're back," he said.

As I closed the tent flap, I heard him begin a story about a dangerous fenrir and a brave pony who saved a girl. Yarra gave a shriek of delight. I hid a smile behind my hand.

In the fortress, the jarl sat at the dice table. She had bathed, and her dark hair hung lose at her shoulders. Aslaug was in their customary position behind her chair. They still wore their armor, though it was no longer splattered in blood. A scribe sat to her left.

I had half-expected to find Ersel with her, in human form, dressed in one of the jarl's gowns. But she was nowhere to be seen. Biting back disappointment, I bowed to Honor and took the chair to her right.

"Ersel left?"

The jarl nodded. "We didn't know how long you'd be gone. Her people swam a long way. She said she wanted to spend the night with her mother. She will find you in the morning."

That made sense. Ersel had always been close to her mother. The merclan wouldn't stay. She needed her chance to say goodbye.

A square piece of vellum was stretched across the table. The scribe had made a list of supplies: bushels of wheat, pounds of meat, axes, and pelts. The jarl pointed to the first line. "I am making a list of provisions that will be sent to you along with the new settlers. My scribe will make two copies. This is a loan. We will expect to be repaid for the goods in three years' time, after the farmers have taken three good harvests." Her eyes crinkled with a smile. "The soil here is good. I expect this town to bring revenue. I return home tomorrow."

"So soon?" I'd expected her to stay at least until the new steward settled.

"The food on the ships will not last long. I will not have my warriors eating what little can be foraged around this settlement."

"And Jarl Ivargar? What if he decides to move in, now that the town is undefended?"

The scribe held up a rolled parchment, tied with a braided golden ribbon and marked with Honor's seal.

"I have written a letter," Honor said. "This settlement is mine. Should he try to take it, I will sack his capital. A jarl who couldn't stand up to a cohort of raiders will not take risks with me."

I scanned the list again. She was sending enough wheat and salt fish to feed a village for months, along with the tools we would need to rebuild houses, fences, and barns. We could round up the loose sheep on the moors. We could trade for broodmares. I could start Mama's line of horses again. Kjorseyrr could prosper.

"This is so much," I whispered.

"As I said, it's a start and will be repaid." The jarl leaned back in her chair and steepled her fingers. "I've invested a lot in you."

She rose from her chair and took Aslaug's arm. "I am exhausted. Let's find a bedchamber."

"I always sleep well in the beds of enemies I have slain," said the húskarl.

Shaking my head, I left them. But instead of going straight to Yarra, I went for a walk. The weights of nostalgia, familiarity, and strangeness all pressed down on me. My legs carried me to the remains of my old house. The roof and most of the walls had been burned, leaving only the stone foundation. I walked to the space that had been my room. The metal chest remained, but it had been flung open and my old clothes stolen. Lief's room had fared better. His bed still stood, black with ash. I knelt beside it. We would rebuild the rest of the town, but I would leave this place as it was. I couldn't live here and I wouldn't erect something in place of my family's memory. A sad smile tugged at my lips. All the construction to come, the remaking of things, would have delighted Lief.

I walked to my tent. Unshed tears stung my eyes, but I was too tired to cry. Yarra was alive. Ersel had come back. The men who had kidnapped me and killed my brother were all dead. It would have to be enough.

A candle in his hand, Smyain stood outside the tent. He cleared his throat, then bent and lifted a shield. "This was left for you. One of Honor's thegns brought it by."

The shield was bright cyan and polished to gleaming. A white, eight-legged horse galloped across its face. I sucked in a sharp breath. The horse's legs almost seemed to move; its mane fluttered in a magical wind. Loki was still here, and they were not waiting to call in their bargain. I had hoped they would give me the winter at least, maybe a year—some time to spend here and rebuild—before taking me away. I should have known better. Loki was close to the freedom they'd desired for centuries. They were not going to wait any longer.

The shield was a warning. Ignoring Loki was a risk I couldn't take. Once the jarl's thegns departed, the Sleipnir could destroy my twenty warriors in a heartbeat. The thought of them feasting on our corpses made my stomach heave. I would have to trust my crew to begin the town's reconstruction without me.

"Give me tonight. At least one night," I hissed and slipped into the tent.

Yarra slept curled under a gray wolf pelt. She hugged her knees to her chest. As quietly as I could, I stripped off my armor and sweaty clothes. One of the men had left a clean tunic and trousers along with a bucket of fresh water. I guzzled some of the water, then used the rest of it to clean myself. Dressed in new clothes, I lifted the pelt and crawled into bed beside my cousin. She wrapped her arms around me in sleep. For this night, we were together again. I would try to forget what was coming in the morning.

Mörsugur
The Bone Month
December

I WAS AWOKEN BY TRYGVE shouting my name. A sword in his hand, he pushed the tent flap aside. "Ragna!"

Without even pausing to rub the sleep from my eyes, I bolted upright and seized my axe from the floor beside our bed of pelts. Had more of Haakon's men been found? Was the Sleipnir running through the camp? Had the Trickster decided that even one night was too much to ask? My gaze darted to Loki's shield. The white horse remained, its silhouette unchanged from last night.

"Enemy ship," Trygve wheezed. "There's an unknown ship sailing toward the harbor."

I closed my eyes and breathed deeply. Human enemies were better than monsters. But where was Ersel? If the rest of her merclan had departed, she could be out in the harbor, alone, when our enemies landed on the beach.

"What is it?" Yarra sat up beside me. Her brown eyes were round with fear. She clutched the wolf pelt in her small hands.

"I don't know," I whispered and smoothed my hand over her hair.

I waved my hook at Trygve, beckoning him inside. "Help me with my armor."

Trygve scooped up the tangle of chain mail and began shaking out the links. I scrambled for my boots and hide braces. The first time raiders had come to Kjorseyrr, I hadn't been prepared. Now, I vowed to always sleep with my fighting gear beside me. I would never be caught unarmed and afraid again. My chain mail was crusted in sweat and dirt. My axe still had brown blood on the blade. I vowed to keep my weapons in better condition too.

Once dressed, I raced to the beach. Many of the jarl's warriors had already assembled there, blocking my view of the harbor. I tried to brush past them, but they were as impregnable as a stone wall. They all stood on tiptoe, craning to see what approached us. None of them acknowledged me.

Torstein pushed his way in beside me. He winked at me. Squaring his massive shoulders, he bellowed, "Get out of the way, you disrespectful bastards! The styrimaðr needs to get through!"

The warriors parted like a gate opening, and, for once, I wasn't annoyed at his loud presence.

He grabbed my arm and tugged me to the front of the crowd. Honor and Aslaug already stood there. The jarl shaded her eyes, focused on a distant ship. Her armor was pristine, without a speck of blood or dust to mar its golden sheen. I wondered if Aslaug had polished it for her, while they sat and talked into the late hours.

"Look," Honor said, pointing across the water.

I followed the line of her arm and swallowed. The ship that coasted toward our shore was not of this world. I had seen merchant vessels from the East with their deep berths, ornamented prows, and proud white sails, as well as the warships favored by sailors from across the North Sea. This ship was not human-made. It was built entirely from silver, with overlapping plates like snake scales. Sixteen metal oars protruded from each of its sides, propelling the titan toward us. The oars moved, but no one sat on the long, gray benches on the ship's deck. Its mast stretched over ten meters high, bearing a wide, black sail. A cloud of cyan mist spilled over its deck and bubbled like boiling water.

"Archers!" Aslaug shouted. The first line of warriors raised their bows and took aim.

"No! Lower!" the jarl countered. She sighed and squeezed my shoulder. "We can't slay a god with arrows."

The great oars stilled. Shrouded by the mist, someone threw a large black anchor over the side of the ship. I scanned the water desperately for Ersel. I wanted time to talk to her, to tell her about the deal I'd made with the Trickster god. I wanted her to sail with me, but I didn't want the invitation to come from Loki's lips.

Heavy chains lowered a small wooden boat into the water. An invisible oarsman rowed it toward us. A golden eagle alit on the boat's prow. It flapped its wings and screeched. Aslaug stepped in front of the jarl and drew their sword.

Dropping my axe in the sand, I walked to the edge of the beach. Torstein started to follow, but I shook my head. "They've come to claim my help," I said. "You heard what I promised them."

Torstein's jaw tightened. "Aye. I did. But I didn't think they would come so soon."

I gestured to the ruined town behind us. "The jarl will appoint her own steward, but I want you to represent me." My gaze dropped to the sand. "I'm trusting you with this. I'm trusting you not to just leave."

"Leave?" Torstein gave a gruff laugh. "You still owe us our weight in gold. I'm not leaving until I get paid."

I chuckled and stepped toward the ocean. The waves lapped at my boots. The rowboat shifted course, moving directly toward me. The eagle tilted its head and clacked its beak. Its eyes were brilliant, electric green. I waited for it to shift forms, to put on a show for the warriors on the beach. But Loki remained in the eagle's body, just waiting. Their eyes never left me. When the boat stopped moving, Torstein dragged it to the shore.

The wall of warriors parted, and a small figure darted through the gap. Yarra stopped in front of me, panting. I knelt in the sand before her. As much as I wanted to take her with me, I had to do what was best for her. I didn't know where the Trickster's ship would take us or how long we would spend searching for the fragments of Odin's dagger. She was still a child. She would be safe here, with the town under Honor's protection.

I looked over Yarra's head to the town behind it. I wanted to rebuild this place, to lead it, and to make that my life's work. But if I didn't go now, the town would have no chance at all. Loki would never forgive me if I broke my bargain with them. And while the dagger existed, my family would always be in danger. The jarls across the sea knew about the dagger now, and they all wanted their chance to make a deal with Loki. When Loki was free and the dagger destroyed, I'd come back to my home for good.

Their weapons poised, the jarl's warriors watched the eagle.

I pulled Yarra to my chest. "I can't take you," I said. "But you'll be safe here now. Safer than you would be with me."

Yarra snorted. "I survived on my own in a cave for months. I think I can handle myself."

"Keep an eye on Torstein for me then, will you?"

Torstein rolled his eyes. He peered down at the little girl. "I will live in terror of your report," he said solemnly.

"I will be back," I said to the eagle. "But I need to talk to someone else first."

The bird gave an almost imperceptible nod.

I stripped off my chain mail and braces, then waded into the surf. The water was freezing, and my clothes dragged. I called Ersel's name softly. She emerged from the water, blue hair falling like a curtain over her face. A relieved sob rose in my throat. I'd known she would wait. She swam to a rock a few meters away and pushed herself onto it. She shifted into her human form, then drew her knees up to her chest.

I paddled to the rock and leaned my elbows onto it. My teeth chattered. "Thank you for what you did, for coming back. I wanted to thank you last night, but the jarl said you were with your mother."

"Yes, I needed to say goodbye," she said. Her blue eyes were trained on the horizon. But if she had already said goodbye to her clan, then she was preparing to stay. We would have a chance to build something together, after all. I could prove to her that I had learned not to take her for granted.

"This isn't exactly how I wanted things to go. I wanted to tell you about Loki before you saw, but they couldn't wait," I babbled. "At least the ship looks spacious. We should have a cabin—"

"I'm not coming with you," she said and finally turned to look at me.

My heart sank like an anchor, right down to the bottom of the sea.

"Are you angry that I summoned Loki? When you were sick? I'm sorry about that. I didn't know what to do."

She shrugged and twisted one of the sea pearls in her hair. "I understand the choice you had to make. If you had sailed with me back to the North Point, you might have lost your chance to win Jarl Honor's favor. Your cousin means a lot to you." She gently lifted my chin so that our eyes were level. "And your revenge meant even more."

"I realized after you left that I didn't treat you fairly," I whispered. My wet hair dripped water down my cheeks, and I was grateful, because it meant she couldn't see that I was crying. "I shouldn't have used you like a weapon. You sacrificed so much for me."

"No," she said, her grip tightening on my chin. "I didn't. Whatever debt you had to me was paid when you sailed back and helped free my people from King Calder. I didn't refuse my king's orders for you. I never wanted to be Havamal's mate if it meant staying in one place... being trapped. Everything I did, all the deals I made with Loki—it was all for me."

"So you forgive me?"

She leaned forward and brushed a chaste kiss over my lips. "I'm always going to feel connected to you. Before I met you, I wasn't brave enough to make my own way. I would have been trapped forever, just waiting for someone else to set a course for me."

"Then why won't you come with me? Is it because of Loki? Will you stay here? Will you wait?" It made sense that she wouldn't want to sail aboard a ship captained by the Trickster. I didn't know how long I'd be away, but if she could wait for me here, help Torstein start to rebuild… This town was on the coast; she wouldn't get sick again.

Ersel pressed her lips together. "When I was a child, the only thing I dreamed about was escaping. I wanted to see the world. I wanted to see humans. You gave me that. But the sea is vast too, and there are so many parts of it I still want to explore. When I almost died, all I was thinking was that it would be a shame if it ended, and I didn't get to see and experience everything I wanted to."

"We'll be navigating the world on Loki's ship." I reached for her hand. "You could see so many things."

"I could see what Loki wants me to see." Reaching under her hair, she undid the knot that held the talisman around her neck. "And afterward, what then? Would I stay here? You *like* command. This is a place you can rebuild and make yours. Maybe someday, I will want one place to call home again, but that isn't what I want right now."

Ersel whispered the incantation to the talisman. The little vial glowed white. She transformed into her kraken form, then slipped into the water beside me. She gently touched my back.

"Loki says I'm selfish," I sniffled. I pushed myself onto the rock and settled in the space she'd vacated. My wet clothes clung to my freezing skin.

"Then so am I, if holding on to dreams is selfish," she said.

She floated alongside me, then reached up to encircle my neck. Her lips pressed against mine. I remembered the day we'd first kissed, when she'd bobbed alongside my little skiff. I'd asked for luck: a mermaid's blessing. She kissed me now with the same hunger we'd shared that day. Her fingers entwined in my hair. She rose a little way out of the water and pressed her body against me. She tasted of salt, and her cheeks were warm where her tears mixed with mine.

If we had rowed out a little farther that day, far enough away that no one would ever find us, would everything that had come afterward have been different? Could I have forgotten my revenge? Could we have been happy exploring the world together?

"When Loki first turned me into this, I saw only one path. I didn't see that I had another option all along. I wanted to spend a lifetime exploring, but I was afraid to go alone." Ersel lifted one of her tentacles out of the water. "But they made me strong. I can crush ships with these. I don't have to be afraid of anything."

I reached into the pouch at my side and drew out the sea pearls I'd taken from her. Her eyes widened and she held out her hand. I gently placed the pearls on her palm, then closed her fingers around them.

"These weren't mine to take," I said.

She combed out a section of blue hair with her fingers, then slid the pearls up the strands.

"Will I see you again?" I asked, my voice shaking. "Will you wait for me to come back?"

Ersel took Loki's talisman and draped it around my neck. The vial pulsed against my skin like a heartbeat, alive with magic and promise.

"One day," she said. "When I have swum across the whole of the sea, and my heart is tired of wandering, I will find you."

Ersel dove under the waves and disappeared.

She would have her freedom at last. I would sail with Loki and return to rule. And even as I sobbed into my arms, I knew that she was right. It was what we both wanted most.

Mörsugur
The Bone Month
December

WHEN MY TEARS SUBSIDED, I swam to the shore. The whole camp had risen to see the ethereal ship floating in the harbor. The jarl was directing her men to load the skiff with basic supplies: salt fish, skins full of fresh water, dry wood. She couldn't spare much, but I was grateful. She'd done so much for us already. I didn't expect Loki to consider my human needs aboard their ship. It could be days until I got the chance to hunt or fish.

Trygve brought an armful of dry clothes. He sniffled as he pressed them into my arms, then hugged me gruffly with one arm. I didn't ask him to go with me. Trygve wasn't a fighter, and there was no one better to watch Yarra. I knew he would look after all the children as well as he had done with me. He would tell them all stories. He would make sure that they had a childhood, no matter what had happened to them. Torstein would have his hands full with construction and organizing the new settlers. They would balance each other.

Taking a deep breath, I stepped into the skiff. I carried my battle-axe in my hand. Loki had not mentioned a fight, but it was better to be prepared. The gods' hatred of each other was legendary. Everyone knew the prediction of the Ragnorak, when they would kill one another at last. With a hatred so deep, Heimdallr would have hidden the pieces of the dagger well. I expected them to be guarded.

I sat on a rowing bench. Heat emanated from an invisible oarsman beside me. My crew pushed the skiff off the beach, and I felt a brush of fabric against my arm. I wondered what kind of enchantment Loki had worked on the crew that kept them invisible. Perhaps the god's ship was crewed by specters of the dead. I swallowed hard. I was going to be alone at sea, with a cruel god and a crew of ghosts. Loki had never promised that I would return from this. I blinked back tears as Trygve hugged Yarra on the beach.

The oars beside me moved. A cloud of steamy breath erupted from the invisible oarsman beside me. Did ghosts breathe? The eagle hopped onto my shoulder and pecked my ear.

Smyain burst through the assembled soldiers. Without hesitating, he plunged into the waves. He grabbed the side of the skip and hauled himself aboard. The eagle ruffled their feathers and squawked at him. Taking no notice of the bird, Smyain sat on the bench opposite me.

"What are you doing?" I demanded.

He shrugged and tugged his tunic over his head. He wrung the water from it. "We all talked. We know you need most of us here, but we decided we didn't want you to go alone."

My eyebrows shot up. "You talked? You all made this decision without consulting me? I am still your captain. What if I wanted to go alone?

He looked down at his hands. "Do you really? I can swim to the beach."

"No," I said quietly. I hadn't been willing to ask any of them to come. It was my bargain and my responsibility. I couldn't guarantee his safety or life. But now that he was here, visible and corporeal beside me, an earnest smile on his face, I wasn't going to turn him away.

I laid my hand on his arm. "But you have to understand—this could take years."

"I'll survive," he said with a grin. "I always do."

The invisible oarsman rowed us across the glassy waves to Loki's ship. When we reached the silver berth, the eagle leapt from my shoulder. Smyain ran his hand along the metal. Up close, the metal plates looked more like feathers than scales, each with delicate silver rachis. The oarsman knocked on the ship's hull and a cyan ladder fell from above.

My legs felt like jelly as I stood. Once I boarded that ship, there was no turning back. I closed my eyes, then eased my foot onto the ladder's first rung. I'd pledged myself to a god, and there had been no turning back from the moment I gave Loki my promise. If I put the people I planned to rule in the path of Loki's creature, how could I be worthy of their support? If I wanted them to follow me, I had to be willing to sacrifice for them.

I stepped onto the ladder, both feet on the rung. The pressure of the air changed, became heavy, as before a storm. I stepped back onto the boat and the pressure eased. Taking a deep breath,

I began climbing. This ship's magic ran deeper than its invisible crew and strange appearance. But whatever awaited us on board, I didn't have a choice. Unless I wanted to unleash the Sleipnir upon my home, my bargain was sealed.

A pale, white hand reached down to help me when I neared the top of the ladder. The Trickster stood on deck, cyan mist swirling at their feet. Their golden eagle feathers had transformed into a radiant sunglow gown that hugged decadent curves. Their raven hair was swept back in a long braid, with eagle feathers tied into the end. Though their face was that of a young woman, their true lips showed through the magic. Loki did not try to hide the black threads binding their mouth. They wanted me to remember our mission.

The god's mysterious crew sat on their rowing benches; they were revealed now that I stood aboard the ship. The nearest to me was a petite woman with jet-black hair and brown skin. She wore a red silk dress and golden arm bands. Next to her was a freckled, ginger boy who wore the black robes of the Gaelic monks. Another man wore a crisp white turban. A dog the size of a wolf rested its head in his lap.

It was a crew from all over the world. Some appeared to be from ancient times. A blonde thegn sat on the bench farthest from me with his eyes trained on the deck. He wore a rich blue tunic with a white trout emblazoned on the front. It was the sigil of the legendary King Forkbeard, who had been dead for over two hundred years. The warrior lifted his eyes to meet mine. Though his face was young, his eyes held a resigned heaviness, as if he had seen too much.

"Who are all these people?" I asked.

"Travellers," said Loki. "People who wished to escape their worlds for a while. I borrowed this ship from the Norns. Everyone on this crew has made their own pact with Skuld or Verðandi. As have I."

The Norns, deities of fate and time, mitigators of debt and sin. They controlled destiny itself. In their hands, time was as malleable as fresh clay. Skuld was the goddess of future and debt. Owe something to her, and one's life became her payment. Verðandi commanded the present time. It was her gift to bestow, and she could take it away. Their sister Urðr commanded fate itself.

Suddenly, I was glad that my bargain was with Loki. The idea that the gods bargained with each other, and were themselves constrained by oath, was new to me. In the politics of the divine, I wondered who owed what and how the economy of promises worked. To get this ship, what had Loki had to bargain? And what had been promised in return?

I ran to the ship's bow. The waves beneath us were barely moving, cresting in slow-motion. On the beach, the people appeared as statues. A bird flew overhead, flying so slowly it was as if it swam in the air. I reached into my pocket and drew out a coin. I threw it into the sea. It moved off my palm in slow motion: a tiny, golden star suspended below the rail.

Loki came to stand beside me, and we watched the coin slowly descend. They laughed as the coin crawled to the sea.

"Time's grasp is more tenuous here in the Neverlands," they said. "We could be gone weeks or years, and, to the people you leave behind, it may seem only days." Their hand moved to my head, and they lifted a strand of my blond hair. Under the sun's glare, it appeared white. "For you, though, you will age with the ship. When you return, you will be different."

"Will I return?" I asked, biting my lip.

The god shrugged. "I guess that depends on your skills. Steer us well, and you'll be back before you turn gray."

They took me by the shoulders and marched me toward the crew. Smyain had taken a seat on the rowing bench beside the man in the turban. The wolf licked his open palm.

"What happens to my crewman?" I asked. "If we run into trouble, I want him to be safe."

Loki frowned. "I did not invite him aboard this ship nor expect him to be here. But he is not bound by any oath. He can leave at any time."

"You don't own his life. If it comes to that, I want your word that he survives."

Loki sighed. "Agreed."

"And you must allow me to command as I see fit. You are a passenger. We are allies." My mouth was dry, and my heart pounded. Loki was a god, but if I didn't establish my position from our first day, they would rule over me. I wanted to lead. If they didn't respect me, Loki would try to trap me in an endless string of deals. If they lost their temper and killed me where I stood, death would end our bargain, and my town would still be safe. I would take my chances.

"We are allies," the god intoned with a roll of their eyes.

"My crew will take breaks. When we are on land, we will hunt and we will feast." I raised my chin, daring them to disagree with me.

Loki stared at me. Their jaw clenched. They turned away from me and barked to the crew. "Line up and meet your new captain."

I hid a smile behind my hand.

Abandoning their oars, the crew scrambled to form a line. I braced my hand on my hip and made a show of inspecting them. I paced between the benches. Smyain gave me an encouraging nod.

I rolled up my sleeves. The woman nearest to me gasped; her eyes were trained on my hook. She winced in what I could only interpret as pity. Once, I might have hidden the hook behind my back. But after everything I had gone through, it was a badge of survival. It was part of me. The woman could pity me if she wanted to. She would learn better soon enough.

I whispered to the markings on my forearm. My toes and fingers went numb. The blood inside me seemed to cool. Even though I could still see my island home and the people lingering on the beach, my tattoos shifted. They showed open ocean before the ship's bow and a path leading to a continent I had never seen on any map.

Loki peered over my shoulder. They traced the path with a long finger.

I pulled my arm against my chest and slowly walked to the ship's bow. Pointing toward the coast, I said, "We sail."

The crew picked up their oars. Loki walked to the stern and raised the black anchor. The sail above us blew taut as a gale of north wind broke through the timespell. We coasted for the stretch of beach ahead. I called directions to the rowers, angling our ship so that we would run aground north of the people still standing on the beach.

My markings still showed only ocean ahead. I had trusted my magic this far, and it was my connection to Heimdallr. Loki's magic had hidden my town in a place that Heimdallr could never find. Maybe my maps showed the world as the god-guardian saw it. If the Norns could build a ship ungoverned by time, what else could it do?

"Are you sure about this?" Smyain called as we neared the coast.

I nodded. The sea breeze rustled through my hair. I stood on the prow and gripped the rail. Would this be the second time I'd steered a ship to disaster? I closed my eyes. A jubilant cheer went up from the crew, as the ship ghosted over the sand.

The End

Glossary

Old Norse Terminology, Gods, and Mythic Creatures

Drekkar—A long, narrow warship with a shallow draft. A drekkar would have space for up to eighteen pairs of oarsmen. It was agile and fast in the water. It was distinct from other light warships in that it always bore a carved prow depicting beasts such as dragons or snakes.

Forseti—The god of justice, revenge, and reconciliation. Forseti belongs to the Aesir gods and is the ceremonial head of the legal court.

Gulltoppr—Mentioned in the *Prose Edda* as the preferred mount of Heimdallr. His name translates to "golden mane."

Haust—The autumn season.

Heimdallr—Known as the guardian of the Aesir gods and the god of foreknowledge or prediction. In myth, Heimdallr has nine mothers and is blessed with exceptional eyesight and hearing. The *Prose Edda* predicts that Loki and Heimdallr will kill each other at the Ragnorak.

Hjarta—Heart.

Húskarl—A bodyguard or warrior in the personal service of a lord or thegn. The actual status of the húskarl varied along with their patron's status. Those attached to nobility could command considerable influence in their own right.

Jarl—A member of the nobility, translated into English as earl. They were the chieftains of a territory; their influence related to the amount of land under their holdings. In some cases, members of the royal family held the title of jarl before ascending to the position of king or queen.

Jotunn—A strong deity that dwells in an alternative realm from the Aesir gods. In early mythology, the Jotnar took many forms, but in later myths, they appear as trolls or giants.

Knarr—A large vessel with a deeper draft, often used by merchants. The knarr had a large sail that allowed it to sail with less dependence on oarsmen.

Loki—The trickster god in Norse mythology. Loki is often portrayed as an instigator or betrayer. In all legends, Loki is shown caring about self-preservation of above all. They can help or hinder, depending on their whim. Loki is genderfluid by canon. Shown in a male form in many legends, they are also described as the birth mother of the Sleipnir and Fenrir.

Norns—Female deities who control human destiny and, in some myths, time. They are usually represented as a trio of giantesses.

Odin—The ruler of the Aesir gods and a being that Vikings considered full of contradictions. He was considered a god of war as well as poetry. He was a ruler who often journeyed far from his kingdom in search of knowledge. He is sometimes referred to as *Alfaðir* or "Allfather" and considered the father of the gods.

Óðinsdagr—Literally "Odin's day" in Old Norse. The Old English equivalent was "*wōdnesdæg*" which became Wednesday.

Ragnorak—An "end of days" event for many Norse gods. It is predicted to culminate in a great battle that will result in the death of several major gods.

Skuld—One of the trio of Norns. Her name means "debt" or "fate."

Sleipnir—An eight-legged, white horse. The Sleipnir is portrayed in the *Prose Edda* as Odin's steed. Loki is described as giving natural birth to the creature.

Snekke—The smallest type of warship and the most common in a Viking fleet. Like the drekkar, it was small and narrow with a very shallow berth. In some cases, its draught was only 0.5 meters. It could carry up to twenty men. They were so light that they could easily be sailed directly onto the beach.

Styrimaðr—A title similar to "captain" that was conferred on the leader of a ship. It means "steer-master" in Old Norse. Unlike the modern role of captain, the styrimaðr often was involved in the physical construction of the ship and was responsible for its maintenance.

Thegn—or *þegn,* was a title given to the retainers of a king or a lord.

Vár—The season of spring. Could also refer to the minor goddess Vár, who was associated with pledges and oaths.

Vaskr—Bold or brave.

Verðandi—Part of the trio of Norns. She is a goddess of time. Her name means "present" or "happening."

Acknowledgments

To the amazing team at Interlude, thank you from the bottom of my heart. You have given me so much support and encouragement as a writer, and you have transformed this duology into books I am so proud of. Annie, your patience and dedication to this story have been crucial. Thank you for talking through so many ideas with me and always listening. Nicki, Cameron and the rest of the editorial team, your insight and attention to detail have been invaluable. Choi, I admit now that when you first described your ideas for the cover of *The Seafarer's Kiss* to me, I was skeptical, but these covers are masterpieces. I didn't think you could outdo yourself for *The Navigator's Touch*, but somehow you have! Candy, thank you for going above the call of duty to promote my books. I am so grateful to you for getting this book in libraries and into the hands of teens.

Thank you:

To Alex, Ava, Chasia and Jen for offering such insightful feedback while this book was in progress.

To Laura, Lizbeth and Rebecca, and so many other amazing people in the Edinburgh-based author community, for providing so much emotional support and letting me bounce ideas off you over a pint at the pub.

To #TeamRocks, Author Mentor Match Fam and the Fight Me Club for giving me space to vent and sharing your knowledge.

To my partner for believing in me when I wanted to give up and for getting me up in the morning to write, even though I am the *worst* before eight a.m. and Diet Coke.

To my family for your constant support over the years and enabling me to pursue a dream.

About the Author

BORN IN CHICAGO, JULIA EMBER now lives in Edinburgh, Scotland with her partner and their city-based menagerie of pets with names from Harry Potter. Sirius Black and Luna Lovegood the cats currently run her life. A world-traveller since childhood, Julia has visited almost seventy countries. Her travels inspire her writing, though she populates her worlds with magic and monsters. She has worked as a teacher, a wedding cake decorator, and a bookseller.

Julia began writing at the age of nine, when her short story about two princesses and their horses won a contest. In 2016, she published her first novel, *Unicorn Tracks*, with Harmony Ink Press. It also focused on two girls and their equines, albeit those with horns. She has subsequently published three further works for young adults.

The Navigator's Touch is the sequel to *The Seafarer's Kiss*, which was released by Interlude Press in May 2017. It was heavily influenced by Julia's postgraduate work in medieval literature at the University of St. Andrews.

Content Warnings

Due to some of the nature of some of the content in *The Navigator's Touch*, I've decided to include this list of chapter specific content warnings for readers who might need them.

General warnings: violence, depiction of kidnapping.

Part 1, Chapter 4

Murder of a child, beating with a belt.

Part 1, Chapter 11

Discussion of torture.

Part 2, Chapter 1

Animal death, graphic depiction of battle injuries.

Part 2, Chapter 4

Depiction of a human-eating monster, graphic execution.

Part 2, Chapter 5

Abuse and imprisonment of children.

an imprint of interlude **press**

@duet**books**

Twitter | Tumblr

For a reader's guide to **The Navigator's Touch** *and
book club prompts, please visit duetbooks.com.*

also from duet

The Seafarer's Kiss by Julia Ember
The Seafarer's Kiss series, Book 1

Mermaid Ersel rescues the maiden Ragna and learns the life she wants is above the sea. Desperate, Ersel makes a deal with Loki but the outcome is not what she expects. To fix her mistakes and be reunited with Ragna, Ersel must now outsmart the God of Lies.

ISBN (print) 978-1-945053-20-7 | (eBook) 978-1-945053-34-4

Not Your Sidekick by C.B. Lee
Not Your Sidekick series, Book 1
2016 Lambda Literary Award Finalist

Welcome to Andover, where superpowers are common — but not for Jessica Tran. Despite her heroic lineage, Jess is resigned to a life without superpowers when an internship for Andover's resident super villain allows her to work alongside her longtime crush Abby and helps her unravel a plot larger than heroes and villains altogether.

ISBN (print) 978-1-945053-03-0 | (eBook) 978-1-945053-04-7

Beulah Land by Nancy Stewart
2017 Foreword Indies Finalist for YA & LGBT Fiction

Courageous teenager Vi Sinclair fights for survival, social justice, and self-defining truth in the forbidding Missouri Ozarks, where, despite her deep-running roots, it's still plenty dangerous to be a girl who likes girls.

ISBN (print) 978-1-945053-45-0 | (eBook) 978-1-945053-46-7